CONTENTS

One Very Smart Bird	1
A Little Neighborly Advice	4
Charlie	6
A Damn Good Pig	12
The Rude Awakening	14
The Hoople Snake	17
Aspirin For A Coon	22
The New Mousetrap	31
Taking The Cure	33
One Upmanship	37
AuSable Poem	38
A Time for Everything - A Time to Doubt	40
Off The Hook	44
Harvest Time For Bears	47
The Saw That Needed New Teeth	53
One Last Dive	56
All That Blood	61
The Window, Part I - The Boogie Man	64
The Window, Part II - The Assassin	67
The Great Goose Farming Operation	69
The Belligerent Bull	71
The Night Time Intruder	77
Christmas In The Prison	82
The Robin	83
The Adventurous Chipmunks	86
Herman	89
The Tomcat And The Bear	101
The Age Old Question	104
The Minnow Thief	106
Old Brownie And Dad	109

Introduction And Credits

"*A*dirondack TALL TALES and SHORT STORIES" is a collection of stories written in a light vein. Many are taken from true incidents from my childhood, while others are stories about incidents told me by my father and those older and wiser then myself about life in the Adirondacks. A few are from the inner workings of an overactive imagination or a cross between reality and fantasy. This book is volume one of a series of Adirondack tall tales and short stories. I sincerely hope you will find a favorite among them.

I am a firm believer that a book of stories is greatly enhanced by good art work. The art work of *Sybil Hedricks* provides the visual concept and helps create the sense of reality that the story conveys. A special thanks to Sybil for her fine art work and imagination in sensing the mood of these tales.

A special thanks to *Art Poppe* of Schroon Lake for the typesetting and for assistance in the cover design.

A very special thanks to *Sue Terry* for her fine work in preparing the art work and locating material to put together this book. Without her help, it would have taken a much longer time.

ONE VERY SMART BIRD
By Fran Betters

*N*ow I've always had a fond regard for nature and believe that animals possess a great deal more intelligence than we humans give them credit for. However, this story I am about to relate comes from my brother, Bob, and I cannot with conscience vouch for its authenticity.

It was one of those real torrid summer days a few years back and we were in the midth of a drought. The streams were real low and all the fish were staying dormant near the bottom in the deeper and cooler water and fishing was pretty much a waste of time since the only thing the fish were interested in was trying to stay alive. Bob was traveling along the old Black Brook road down by the flats near the Crowly farm and happened to look out into the field. He saw a large blue Heron standing in the middle of the field with its head down. Now, most of the time when you see a blue Heron, it is standing on a rock in the stream or flying over the river in an attempt to locate a fish for dinner. This particular bird was just standing still in the large field and Bob was curious to see what it was doing there. He stopped his pickup truck alongside the road to observe the bird more closely. Suddenly he saw the bird make a quick movement with its foot and then reach down and pick up something with its beak. It then took off and flew across the highway in front of Bob's truck, and then flew over the stream alongside the highway. The bird circled a couple of times until it was over a particularly fishing looking spot on the stream and then dropped whatever it was holding into the water. Quickly grabbing a pair of binoculars from the seat, Bob was able to locate the object the bird had dropped. It was floating on the currents of the stream and Bob could see it was a large grasshopper. The grasshopper floated for about fifty feet in the currents before a small trout rose from the bottom to take the insect. Just as the fish rose to take the grasshopper, the blue Heron dove down and grabbed the fish in its beak.

Bob says he couldn't believe what he was seeing so he sat back and waited to see what the bird would do next. After eating the small fish, the blue Heron circled back over the field and landed in almost the exact spot where it had gotten the grasshopper. Bob continued to watch as the bird repeated the procedure, capturing another grasshopper and then flying back over the river to drop it in the currents, then diving to take the fish when it rose for the grasshopper. Bob watched for another half hour while the blue Heron repeated this procedure two more times. Then having satisfied it's appetite, the bird flew off across the river and disappeared.

Bob then told me the bird had been so successful that he had gone back home, got a glass jar and had collected a bunch of grasshoppers, and then had gone back to fish the pool. He says he only caught two fish, proving that the bird was a better fisherman than he was. I was quick to agree with him.

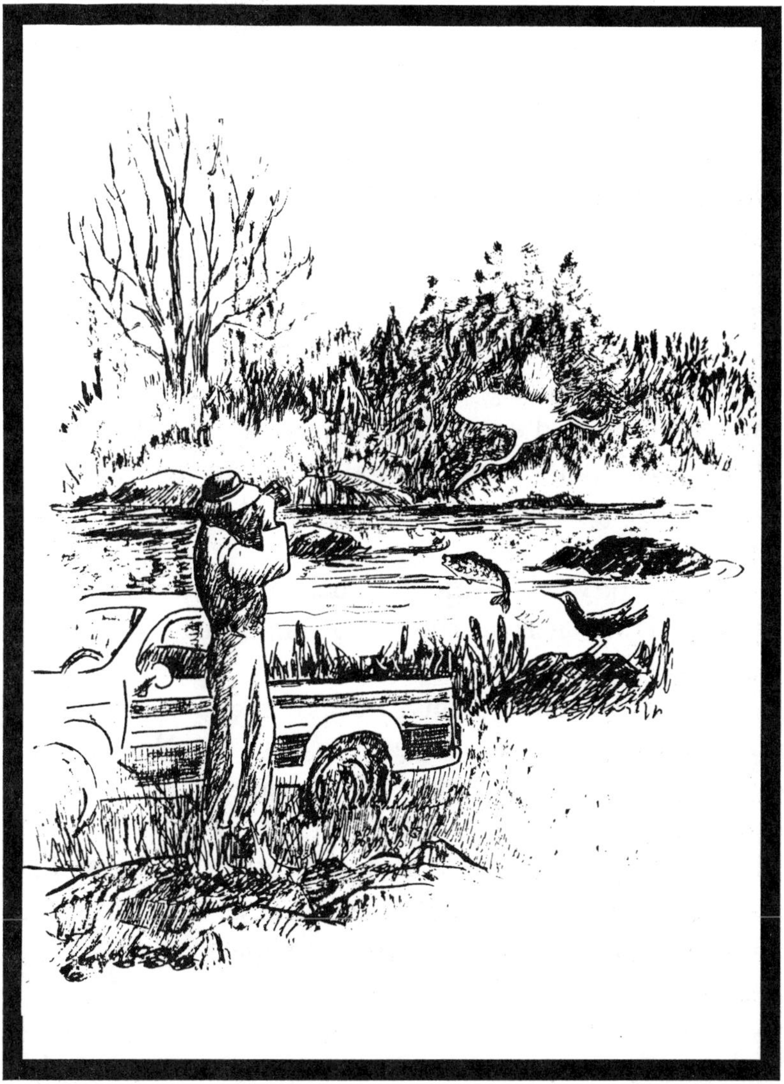

A LITTLE NEIGHBORLY ADVICE
By Fran Betters

Some many years ago, an old Adirondack farmer who lived outside the small village of Bloomingdale, was known for his wit and quick thinking. One day, another farmer from across the lake in Vermont, purchased a little piece of land next to the old man, and with a couple of horses and a few chickens, attempted to scratch out a living. Their land was adjacent to each others and as they plowed the fields, they would eventually stop and chat for a bit on the rare occasions they came together at the end of a furrow.

One day while having such a chat, the new farmer from across the lake lamented on how expensive horse feed was and he'd be danged if he knew how a man could feed his horses now that the price of feed had risen. Now, the Adirondack settler saw an opening and was quick to take advantage of it. Pushing back his old felt hat, he looked the other straight in the eye and replied. "well, I've been able to cut my feed bill in half in the past six months and my horses are doing fine". The new comer looked up from the furrow with a keen interest now and inquired. "Just how did you go about that, if I may ask?" "well", the Adirondacker went on, "I just set about to mixing a little sawdust in with the oats, just a little at first, mind you, and noticed that the horses didn't seem to mind. I started increasing the amount of sawdust a little bit at a time until I got them eating a fifty percent mixture of sawdust and oats. As you can see, my horses are doing just fine". The new farmer never noticed the glitter in the old man's eye as he clapped the harness against his horses flanks and started making another furrow back toward his farm house.

The old settler didn't see the new comer again until about six months later when he was out in the fields planting his spring crop of potatoes. He saw the new farmer across the field and when he came to the end of the row he was planting, shouted across to him. "How are your horses doing on their new formula?". The new farmer looked up and replied with a sad voice. "Well, you know that advice you gave me worked out just fine. I had them horses eating a good mixture and was all the way up to where they were eating about ninety percent sawdust and ten percent oats, when they both up and died on me. I just don't know what did happen to um, but I sure appreciated the advice. It sure did save me a lot of money".

CHARLIE
By Fran Betters

I suppose that there will be some skeptics as to the veracity of this story but there are a number of witnesses living here in Wilmington that can swear to everything in this story - and prove once more that truth is indeed stranger than fiction, and that animals are often much smarter than we humans give them credit for.

It was twenty five years ago that I first met Edna and Carl Broquist, a young couple that had just recently purchased the Viking restaurant - just outside the village of Wilmington along Rt. 86. This place is now called the Wilderness but at that time it was "The Viking" and as still is, one of the restaurants in the region known for it's excellent food.

Edna was a vivacious little lady with a ready smile and a quick wit and her husband, Carl, was the typical friendly bartender who also possessed a good sense of humor and was an excellent conversationalist.

From the very beginning, I became very good friends with them both and spent many enjoyable hours having many friendly drinks and conversations at their place. It was also an insight into the many fine qualities of Edna's personality that manifested itself to her many friends. The one trait however, that we found the most unusual was her affinity for animals. Not just the domestic variety such as dogs and cats, but the wild animals that often came by their place to visit and explore the garbage cans at night or perhaps just pass through the woods on the opposite side of the highway.

Before I get on with the real story, let me just relate one incident that will give the reader an insight into her particular ability to equate with all types of animals. Outside the kitchen of the restaurant was a large garbage can with the lid which often lay loosely across the top of the can. One evening when she, her husband, my friend George - also a frequent visitor to the bar and a good conversationalist, and myself were involved in one of our philosophical discussions, we heard a noise outside the kitchen door coming from the vicinity of the garbage can. We went outside to check and saw that the cover was off the can and there was a scratching noise coming from inside the can, indicating that some sort of animal had fallen into the can and was unable to climb out. Before anyone else could get over to the can, Edna quickly went over and checked the can. Finding a skunk inside, she casually reached inside and lifted it out, holding it like a kitten and it made no effort to spray or in any way indicated any fear from this person. She gently put the skunk down on the ground and petted it gently at the same time speaking to it in a gentle voice as it waddled off into the woods alongside the building, while we watched with trepidation and slightly held breath in anticipation of the strong odor that didn't materialize.

It was the following spring that our real story began. One day Edna went out to one of the cabins that they rented out behind the Viking. Lying on the ground beneath one of the large pine trees was a small song bird with a broken wing. It had obviously fallen out of its nest and was in bad shape. This of course was a challenge and the good samaritan in her decreed that she could do nothing more than take the bird inside and nurture it back to health. Little did she realize what a bonding friendship she would be nurturing. She named the bird Charley, and with her tender care and feeding, it was soon strong and healthy and able to fly on its own again. But the bird did not go off on its own to forget about it's adoptive mother. It continued to stay around the property and each time Edna would call "Charlie", the bird would always appear somewhere from it's perch in one of the trees and fly down to land in Edna's hand. The bird seemed to grow fonder and fonder until it would ride around inside the restaurant on Edna's head while she was working around the place.

It seemed that each time the bird flew off to some destination that it might not return but this was not the case, for the following day when Edna would call "Charlie", in a short time the bird would come flying from over the tree tops and suddenly appear to light on her hand. It would then allow itself to be taken inside where it would perch for an hour or more on her head or wherever she wanted it to stay.

This amazing friendship between human and bird led to some interesting and humorous conversations when ever someone from the city or an unknown customer would stop in at the bar for a drink. Needless to say, there were many doubtful stares and comments made when Edna would announce that it was time to go out and call Charlie. The looks on the Doubting Thomases would change to incredibility when the bird flew from out of nowhere regardless of the time of day or night and come to land on her hand.

Everyone who knew of this relationship thought that come fall, when the birds headed south, that it would be the last we would see of Charlie, but this was not the case. Charlie left with some other birds sometime in October and Edna was about the only one who had confidence that the bird would return in the spring.

It was near the end of April the following spring when Edna went outside the kitchen door and called "charlie". It was a beautiful spring day and with the utmost confidence, she waited patiently for about five minutes and as if on cue, the bird appeared as it had so many times the previous summer, and landed in her outstretched hand.

That fall the bird once more flew South with its friends and again the following spring, it returned at about the same time. For the next two years, Edna and Charlie spent many hours in each other's company and provided a raft of good conversation and discussions regarding the intelligence of our non-human friends. The third winter that it went South, it did not return and only the fates could have intervened to prevent Charlie from returning to his friends in the Adirondacks and to spend another summer with Edna.

11

A DAMN GOOD PIG
By Fran Betters

Some years back while traveling through a small rural town, I was unfortunate enough to have my car break down along a dirt road near an old farm house. Unable to determine the cause of the problem, I walked back to the farm house and up the driveway in hopes that they might allow me to use the phone to call the nearest garage. Just before reaching the front porch, I noticed a pig pen off to the side of the driveway. Closer observance revealed a most unusual sight. Inside the pen stood a full sized pig with a wooden leg. Since I had never seen a pig with a wooden leg before, I stood for a minute and stared before continuing on to knock at the front door. A moment later, the door was opened by a nice looking lady in her mid thirties. After explaining my problem and asking if I might use the phone, she cordially invited me in and pointed the way to the phone on a small desk in the corner of the room. With the number she gave me, I was able to reach a nearby garage and was assured that they would send someone out right away. After putting the phone down, I turned to the woman to thank her for letting me use the phone. I remembered the pig outside and casually commented on how unusual it was to see a pig with a wooden leg. She grinned and replied "Mister, you don't know how unusual that pig really is. About a year ago, my husband and I and our two children were asleep upstairs and during the night, a fire broke out in the kitchen behind the wood stove. That pig smelled the smoke and broke out of his pen and pushed open the front door and awoke us. We were able to put out the fire and if it hadn't been for that pig, we might have all burned to death".

The lady had just finished telling me this when her husband entered the front door. I explained my presence and mentioned that his wife had just told me about the pig saving them from the fire. He excitedly replied "That's only half the story. She didn't tell you about the time last fall when I was plowing out there in the field. The tractor tipped over and pinned me face down in the dirt. I was smothering and couldn't get out from under it. That darn old pig broke out of his pen and raced across that field and dug me out with his feet. I'd have died for sure if it hadn't been for that pig".

Flabbergasted, I was finally able to stammer. "But how come the pig has a wooden leg?". His reply was even more startling. "Mister, when you got a pig that good, you don't eat him all at once".

THE RUDE AWAKENING
By Fran Betters

I was a young lad in school at the end of world war two and my cousin Milton had just returned from fighting in Italy. He loved to hunt and this was to be his first hunting trip since returning home from the war and my father, also an avid hunter, spent many days hunting the large mountains behind our home in the country. It was on one such deer hunting outing late that season when the following incident took place.

There was about eighteen inches of snow on the ground, and as I recall, there was only a couple of days left in the deer season. Milton and my father planned to hunt the big valley on the back side of Hickok mountain. They left the house at dawn that morning and trudged through the heavy snow on the top of Hickok and then down the other side. At the top of the mountain, they had separated to make a large circle back towards each other in the hope of driving a deer to the other one. They had been hunting in this manner for a couple of hours and my father knew that they must be approaching each other when he heard a loud and excitable shout from Milton. He stopped in his tracks and stared in concentration in the direction from which the sound had come, hoping to see a deer bounding in his direction. After waiting a reasonable time, and not seeing anything, he continued onward and a few minutes later encountered Milton, who was standing shaking the snow from his hunting cap.

When my father approached him, he said Milton was as white as a ghost. Milton pointed down at the snow and there in the snow besides his own footprints were the footprints of a large bear. Milton explained that he had stepped over a large log and had stepped right on top of the bear, that had hibernated up against the log before the snow storm. When he had stepped on the bear, it had awakened and taken off on a dead run. Milton had been shaken and had started running also. After running for a hundred feet or more, Milton turned to see the bear running right along side him. At this point, he and the bear decided to change course, Milton lost had lost his hunting cap and had to go back and retrieve it.

They both had a good laugh and my father asked him what he had said to the bear when he turned and saw the bear running along beside him. Milton's reply was quite revealing of his predicament. "I said, move over and let someone run who knows how". Later on, my father asked him why he hadn't shot the bear and he had another good answer. I was too close and I was afraid the bear would take the gun away from me if I pointed it at him". This story has been told many times over the years to the hunters my father guided in those same mountains.

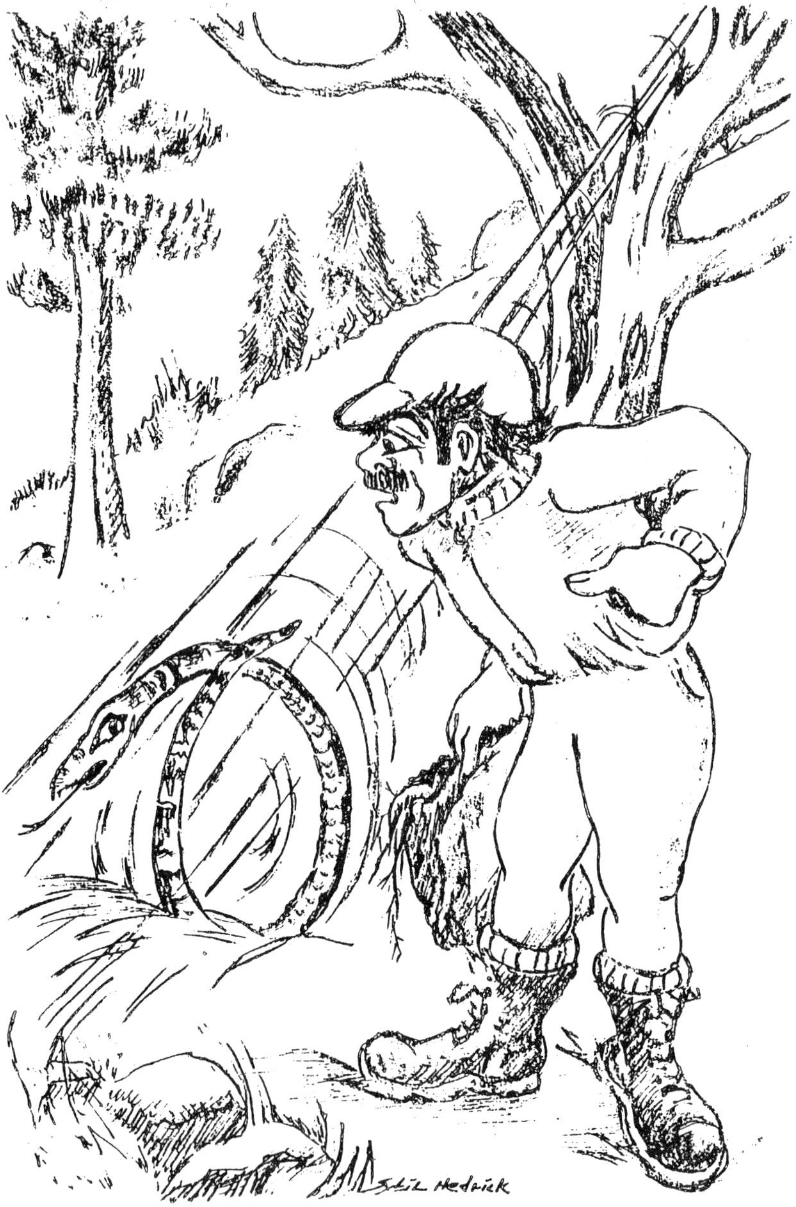

THE RARE AND ELUSIVE ADIRONDACK HOOPLE SNAKE
By Fran Betters

*M*y home was a two story farm house a few miles outside the little village of Wilmington, and my back yard was the woodlands and logging trails that led up the side of nearby Hickok mountain. From the time I was about nine years old until I graduated from high school, this territory became as familiar to me as the house I lived in. My dad was a well known hunter and fisherman, and I was taught during my early formative years to respect the woods but not to fear them. I was also taught to respect the many creatures that made the woods their home. Deer, grouse, rabbits and even bear were not an uncommon sight, and by the time I was twelve or thirteen, I had explored all of Hickok mountain and knew all about the hidden springs, the caves and even the ledges near the top where a movie company had once filmed a mock battle before my time. As I grew older and into my teens, like all lovers of nature, I became enraptured with the huge mountain behind Hickok mountain. It was named Stuart mountain and my father had often cautioned me not to go over the other side of that mountain. From the base of the mountain on that side, there were miles of swamp and one could travel for a distance of about seventeen miles before coming to another road.

In my teen years when I was given my first hunting rifle, I began to explore Stuart mountain and would often envision the time when I could venture down that forbidden side and into the swamps to hunt what was called the

Marsh pond region. It was in this area that my father had once killed a huge sixteen point buck that had dressed out at three hundred and three pounds, when I was about ten years old. I can still remember vividly the sight of that huge deer hanging from the limb of the large old pine tree behind the woodshed.

I grew older with the years and eventually hunted those big swamps on the other side of Stuart, and I met animals I had not encountered previously in the not so remote sections of the mountain. I once saw a whole family of Fishers cavorting about on the mountain side as I watched from beneath a overhanging precipice a hundred yards farther up on the mountain. On one occasion, I had observed a mother Bobcat with her kittens racing off in the distance. Once I had a large red fox walk with his head down within a few feet of me as I sat silently on an old decaying log partially hidden in a small clump of spruce. I can see the startled expression on the fox's face when I greeted him with "Hello, Fox". He did a full 360 degree turn in mid air and was running at full speed in the opposite direction when his feet hit the ground. It was the only time I have every known of anyone getting that close to a full grown fox, as they are by nature the most cautious of creatures.

Those were the best year of my life, growing up in that old farm house with the love and teachings of a very special mother and father. Those years in and around the woods continuously reinforced my father's decree to respect all of nature's creatures, and I came to believe that I had seen the full array of inhabitants that lived in those mountains and swamps.

It was many years later, about thirty in fact, that I learned that there was one creature that lived in the high peaks of the Adirondack mountains that I had never seen, or even knew of its existence. By this time, I was the owner operator of a large sporting goods business on the banks of the famous AuSable river. I spent many hours on the stream teaching fly fishing, and although I still loved the mountains, rarely found the time to get back into the more remote sections where I had ventured as a teenager.

One day an older gentleman moved into our village and eventually found his way into my shop. I found him to be a most interesting individual. He was extremely knowledgeable about many subjects and had spent most of his eighty plus years hunting, trapping and exploring the woods. It was inevitable that we become good friends. After a few years, as this friendship deepened, he would often hang around the shop for hours telling stories about the good ole days and about his many escapades, to the delight of myself and other sportsmen who happened to be in the region. It came as a complete surprise however, when one evening while sitting in my favorite rocking chair in my house attached to the shop, that he asked if I had ever seen the rare Adirondack Hoople snake in my years of living in the high peaks region. Noticing the surprised expression on my face, he gave me his trademarked two tooth grin on his grizzled weather beaten face and went on to tell me the following story.

He claimed he was about three miles back into the mountains one late fall day and was searching for Ginseng, a plant that when dried and ground, is purported to have aphrodesiac properties. Well, anyway, he was looking for this plant on the shaded north side of the mountain on a high ridge near the top. He had found a few of the smaller plants and was pushing the decayed matter around on the forest floor looking for larger roots, when he put his hands into a thick nest of twigs and leaves that was about three feet in diameter. He heard a hissing noise and quickly pulled his hand back. He had uncovered a large nest that contained four of the most beautiful little snakes he had ever seen. He stated he had never seen any snakes before with such strange markings and was curious as to what kind they might be. Taking a small stick that he found on the ground nearby, he began to poke around at the nest and was greatly surprised to see the snakes, which were about twelve inches long, coil themselves into a perfect hoop and go rolling off down the mountain side. He said the snakes had pronounced vermiculations on them much the same that a brook trout has. He had wanted to study them closer but they disappeared so fast that he didn't have a chance to further observe them. He thought no more of it, and stored the experience in the back of his mind while he continued to hunt the region for more Ginseng roots.

After finding and collecting a brown shopping bag full of the most sought after roots, he began his descent down the mountain. After climbing down a particularly steep ravine, he stopped and leaned back up against a medium sized tree about twelve inches in diameter to rest for a spell.

He had been resting only a couple of minutes when he heard a loud whooshing noise and turned just in time to see a large snake about six feet in diameter coming at a tremendous speed down the mountain, directly at him. A split second before the snake would have hit him, he stepped away from the tree, and the snake hit that twelve inch tree dead center splitting it as cleanly as if someone had sliced it in two with a huge knife. The snake just continued on down the mountain and out of sight. He estimated the speed at which the snake was traveling at about a hundred miles an hour. He claimed that as the snake went by him, he noticed a mean, demon like expression on the snake's face and it seemed to stare directly at him. He got the erie feeling that it was telling him "Don't mess with my children again". With a cold chill creeping up his spine, he made his way down to the base of the mountain and back to his cabin, all the while keeping an eye out for a return encounter with the large hoople snake. He related that after the experience, when ever he was in the mountains, he would look for trees that had been split by hoople snakes. He told me where two were located if I ever wanted to go and look at them. I graciously declined saying it was best not to know about certain things. We never discussed the subject again.

AN ASPIRIN FOR A COON
By Fran Betters

When I first opened my sporting goods business over twenty years ago along the banks of the famous AuSable River in the little village of Wilmington, the land where I built my shop was nothing but large pines standing nearly sixty feet high and some of them over two feet in diameter. I thought it would be both economical and practical if I cut down the trees and had them sawed into lumber to build my store. It turned out to be much less expensive than buying the lumber outright. When I finished the cutting project, I had about eight thousand feet of excess lumber which I sold back to the lumber mill. There was only one drawback to my plan, or I made one mistake which once was made was never to be corrected . . for once you cut down a tree, there is no way to put it back. After building my store and getting everything set the way I wanted it or should I say, what I could afford, I began to have second thoughts about cutting all the trees behind where my shop was situated, back to about 800 feet. I was now left with a fair sized empty lot. After some thought, I decided that it could best be utilized by putting in a small block of buildings for showers and toilets and adding some fireplaces and some picnic tables and water fawcets and turn the whole thing into a nice little campground. I decided to give my campers plenty of space, so I made room for only 18 sites and the whole thing worked out quite nicely.

I operated the campsite along with my sporting goods store for about seven or eight years until my sporting goods store grew to the point where I didn't want to be bothered with the campsite anymore. It was also difficult to find capable and dedicated help, so I finally closed the campground part of the business. I must confess however; I missed a lot of my steady campers that came every year and during those times when the campsites were operating I had many good laughs and met lots of interesting people from around the country.

Since my business is located outside the village area, and pretty much isolated from the town tourists and other businesses, my campers were treated to quiet and peaceful solitude with the AuSable River bordering one section of my property and two sides hemmed in by woods. There were those times, not all that infrequent, when they were treated to the sight of a deer wandering across the camping area to the woods on the opposite side, and most of the time there were families of chipmunks and squirrels scurrying about the area. A couple of times a bear would venture into the camping area but would usually be scared away by the campfires or some woman letting out a loud screech at anything that sounded like it might be a bear. The one incident that I remember the best concerns a family of Raccoons that frequented the camping area for a period of about three years. This family consisted of a very large mother coon and three smaller coons which became quite tame. Many of the repeat campers came to know them and liked having them around even though they could become pests at times. The old mother coon got to be friendly to the extent that she would often come up to the door of my sport shop late at night when I was tying flies and peek in. I could get her to take food from my hand but never could reach out and pet her. If my hand got a little too close she would hiss at me and back away. I guess you might say she was a firm believer that "familiarity breeds contempt" so I didn't pursue the matter too vehemently.

One September afternoon, however, when the campground was not too busy and the weather had began to turn a little on the cool side, a nice young black couple from the Montreal area came into my shop and purchased some fishing gear and after talking for a spell about the great fishing in the area, I had convinced them they should spend the weekend in the area. The girl was a vivacious young lady with a sparkling personality and she explained that they were on their honeymoon and seemed excited at the prospect of spending a weekend camping out and go fishing. With her urging and enthusiasm they decided to stay over for a weekend. After paying me the camping fee, I sent them back to what I considered one of my nicer and little more remote camping spots near the woods, with the admonition to not be afraid to call me if I could assist them in any manner over the weekend. The one thing I forgot to do was remind them that they might hear animals like squirrels or raccoons around the camping area during the night.

    The next morning being a weekend, I was in my shop bright and early tying up some flies and waiting for the first customer to come in. It was only about six-thirty and I could tell by the clear blue sky and the bright sunrise that it was going to be an exceptional fall day and by two in the afternoon there would be some good hatches of mayflies on the river. This time in September was always exceptional fly fishing and I knew that the few campers, most of which were fishermen, would have a good day on the stream. I also looked forward to a busy day with lots of the regular customers driving up from cities such as Syracuse, Albany, Utica, etc.

    Since most of the campers did not rise early at this time of the year, I was somewhat surprised when the lovely black newlywed walked in through the open door of my shop with a cheery "good morning". I responded likewise and commented that they were going to have a beautiful day and would have no trouble catching a nice trout dinner. Her response was "that's great, I'm looking forward to it. My husband is cooking breakfast and I thought I'd come up and pick your brain to find out what's best to use for those tasty trout." I was about to answer her and give them the benefit of my stream experience when, with a big smile, she exclaimed "and by the way, did a big coon come up here and ask for an aspirin this morning?"

As I looked directly at her, she must have noted a somewhat shocked expression on my face, and with a tilt of her head backwards she laughed and exclaimed "No, not my husband, not that kind of coon, I mean those four legged burglar face coons." She then went on to explain that sometime during the early morning hours, she heard a noise inside the fly of their tent which they had set up over the picnic table. She got up and peeked out and on the table was mama coon in the process of stealing a bag of flour they had left the previous evening. She explained that she had reached out through the tent flap and grabbed a small frying pan that was sitting on the seat of the table and gently bopped Mama coon on the head. She was quick to add, "I didn't hurt her, but she quickly left without the flour." I just thought she might have a little headache this morning." I laughed with her and told her about the family of coons that hung around most of the time. She responded "If I see Mama again this evening, I'll apologize and give her one of the fish I'm going to catch." About this time her husband came walking around the corner into the shop with a smile and friendly "good morning" and turning to his bride, told her that breakfast was ready. I told them to go have breakfast and then stop back in and I would set them up with the proper bait and tell them a couple of productive spots where they were sure to catch some trout.

As they walked out and back down to their campsite, I reflected that they made a nice couple and that he was lucky to have a girl with such an outstanding personality and sense of humor along with confidence. She hadn't said, "I'll give Mama coon one of my fish IF I catch one", but had stated, "I'll give Mama coon one of my fish I AM GOING to catch". I've always been partial to people with a positive attitude towards life and I determined that I would do my best to steer them in the right direction on their first trip to fish my favorite stream.

Over the next hour and a half, I waited on about a dozen customers selling them the proper flies to match the hatches of Isonychia Bicolors that would be hatching off the streams later in the day. They walked back in as I was picking out a half dozen of the big imitation nymphs for one of my regular customers and stood along side the large glass case containing the thousands of flies and seemed fascinated with the buggy imitations I had lying on the counter and with the advice I was dispelling on how to fish them. After that customer had paid me and left the shop, I spent the next twenty minutes explaining to them about Mayfly hatches and about the nymph stage of the flies and answered their many questions about fly fishing techniques. They both had light action spinning rods and explained that they had never fly fished before but thought it was very fascinating. I explained that it was more difficult to fly fish with a spinning rod but it could be done.

I gave them each two of the big imitation nymphs and showed them how to tie them on and apply a section of wrap-around lead about 12 inches above the fly to get it down under the water. After explaining that they should cast into the currents and let the fly drift down and then retrieve it with short, quick jerks as the real fly was a fairly fast swimmer. I also explained that the best time was during the afternoon hours, but if they fished the fly a little deeper and in the deeper pools, they could probably pick up a few trout before then. After waiting on a couple more customers, I then drew a map telling them how to get to one of my favorite fishing spots. With their enthusiasm I had the feeling they would catch fish and that I would be helping to introduce two more likely candidates into the social world of fly fishing.

I did not see them again that day until just before dark, which near the end of September is about five o'clock. Anyone present in the shop when they came in would have thought they had just won the New York State Lottery. She was carrying the inexpensive canvas fishing creel they had purchased the previous evening and they were both spilling over with eagerness, both talking at the same time telling me what a great day they had. All the while they were talking, she was pulling the trout out of the creel and laying them on a newspaper she had been holding in her other hand and placed the fish on the counter for me to see. There was a total of six fish and the largest was 14 inches. A nice respectable catch of trout for even the experienced anglers. They both confessed they had never cleaned a fish before, so I took them into my kitchen (my house is attached to the back of my sport shop) and cleaned the trout showing them how to do it. Taking three cold bottles of beer from the frig, I handed each a bottle and toasted to their success on the stream, and to a happy marriage.

That evening they cooked their trout over the open campfire and true to her word, she left the smaller of the trout for Mama coon to enjoy later that night.

The next day they purchased two inexpensive but well balanced fly rod outfits and spent the rest of the weekend exploring and enjoying the Adirondacks.

I didn't just gain two new customers that day but two very good friends that have been coming back to this area to fish every summer for two weeks each time. They both took my fly fishing seminar the following summer and are now both experienced and dedicated sports people. They met the river and both they and the river have benefited from their mutual acquaintance. Both Sam and Barbara are now in the process of teaching their six-year-old son the basics of fly fishing so my list of customers and friends continues to grow.

A THOUGHT

A thought is like a flower
That blossoms in the night
And in the light of early dawn
May give us much delight

THE NEW MOUSETRAP
By Fran Betters

*T*wenty five years ago I bought five acres of land along the banks of the AuSable river and with the help of a friend, cut down the large pine trees and had them sawed into lumber. With this lumber, I built a sport shop where I tied custom flies, made custom rods and opened a fly fishing school. The shop had a full sized basement that came in handy for many different purposes. I had a bed there so I could stay overnight at the shop, a counter to work on and much storage area for rods, materials etc. There was also one other purpose for which this basement became quite well known by some of my local friends. When I was a young lad, my mother used to make old fashioned home brewed beer for my father and home made root beer for me. I became familiar with the procedure and was not about to let this knowledge go to waste. There was a store in nearby Saranac Lake where I could buy the necessary ingredients such as malt, hopps etc. and I had salvaged an old bottle capper from the old house so I began making home brew for myself and a few choice friends. Now, one thing I remember well about the home brew making was that my mother would add a small teaspoon of sugar to each bottle before capping it. The capped bottle of the brew would then be set in a warm place to ferment the brew and later put in a cool place to age for the proper time. Sometimes when a little too much sugar was added, the bottles that my mother stored in the pantry behind the old wood stove would work a little too much and occasionally explode. This was always an exciting time in our house when a bottle, sometimes two or three, would explode. I

I was soon to learn that this unique problem would be carried over to her son in his endeavors to make a good but potent brew. One particular bath of brew became quite well advertised and is still talked about by some of those who witnessed the invention of what later was called the new Better's mouse trap. This particular batch was brewed pretty much the same as others I had made only I had inadvertently put in a little too much sugar before capping. It was also a late fall day when I bottled it and the gas stove I had in the basement was working with high efficiency. The brew was left to work and at the proper time lapse, my brother Bob and another friend just happened to drop by at the shop and the offer was made to sample the new batch of brew. We all proceeded down the stairs to the basement and eyed the line of bottles waiting to be sampled. As Guy Stephenson, our friend, walked across the floor, he looked down to see a bottle of brew that had exploded and lying along side the bottle was a large mouse with a shard of glass through its body. When the bottle exploded, It had killed the mouse that just happened to be walking across the basement floor. As I reached down to grab a bottle to hand to Guy, another bottle exploded before it could be opened. We managed to salvage a few good bottles but Guy would always remark later when ever someone mentioned home brew. "It was like drinking beer in a mine field". Then someone would add. "I know but Adirondackers are a tough breed, they don't shy away from danger".

TAKING THE CURE
By Fran Betters

For the past twenty five years, I've owned and operated a large sporting goods business and during the months from April until the end of October, my work days are twelve to fifteen hours long taking care of customers. From November until April, however, my time is pretty much my own. So a few years back, a good friend and fishing buddy asked me if I would do him a favor. He had purchased a bar, and being a full time corrections officer, he needed someone to operate it for him while he was working, during the winter months.

I had tended bar before and had also managed a large restaurant complex in the village where I lived, so I thought this would be a fun thing to do, while at the same time, doing a favor for a friend.

The job led to many new friendships and also to some new experiences. There were many laughs along with a number of amusing incidents, but the following will stick in my memory as the main event of that winter's experience.

It was one of my slow afternoons in the bar and my only customer at the time was a guy I'll call Joe. Now Joe was known to imbide quite frequently and you could usually find him in the place every afternoon. He was a friendly guy and never caused anyone any problems. When he had a little too much to drink, he would put his head down on the bar and quietly take a little nap. I

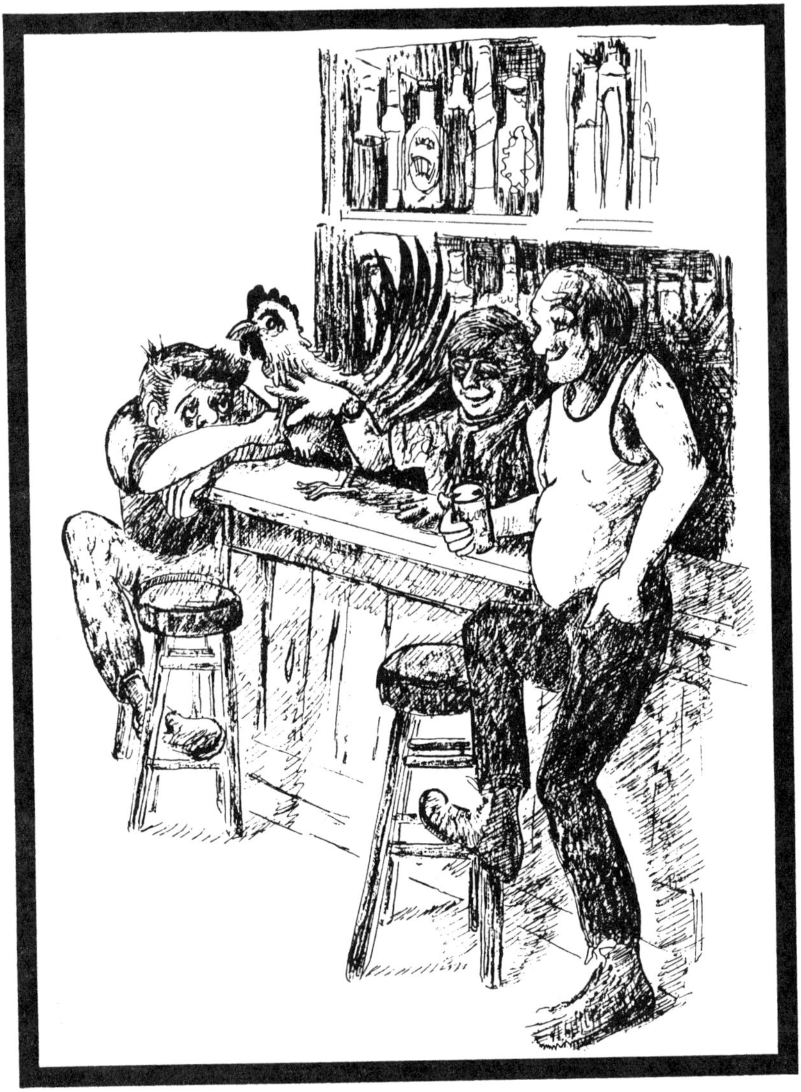

usually ignored him and let him sleep it off until he awoke and was ready to walk back to his home across the street from the bar.

    This particular afternoon, he was taking his usual nap after too many beers, when another customer and friend walked in and took a seat at the bar. I'll call him Buddy because that happened to be his name. Now, being a professional fly tyer, I had mentioned to Buddy some time before that I could use some good neck hackle from his rooster to tie dry flies. Well, it just happened that this particular afternoon, Buddy brought to the bar with him one of his most prized roosters. It was a very large and beautiful bird, and Buddy stood petting this large rooster when Joe awoke from his nap. With blurry eyes, he looked up and saw the rooster and said in a slurred voice "Whats that rooster doing in here?". Both Buddy and I ignored him. Joe rubbed his eyes and again in a slurred voice, repeated "Whats that rooster doing in here?". This time I looked over at Joe and replied "Joe, that's not a rooster, it is one of my customers, now please don't bother him". Joe put his head back down on the bar and a few minutes went by while I continued to look the bird over checking its neck hackle for dry fly quality - all the while petting the bird's back and neck. Again Joe lifted his head from the bar and rubbed his eyes and asked "Whats that rooster doing in here?". Buddy didn't say a word, just grinned as I walked over to Joe, put my hand on his shoulder and said quietly. "Joe, if you don't stop bothering my customers, You'll have to leave. Now that is not a rooster, its one of my customers". Joe rubbed his eyes a couple of times, got up on wobbly legs and walked on out of the bar. We could hear him muttering to himself as he clumsily made his way out the door. All we could make out was "it sure looks like a rooster to me".

Joe would continue to make his usual appearance at the bar each day but I never saw him drink anything after that except ginger ale. I would often remark to Buddy afterwards that he should rent out his rooster to Alcoholics Anonymous. It provided us with a good laugh and my friend Jack, who owned the bar, is still telling this story about the rooster that cured Joe.

ONE-UPMANSHIP
By Fran Betters

To many an old Adirondack settler, the only real assets they possessed were their little cabin or farm house, their animals and the farm land itself. This is the story of one such adirondack settler who had lived his entire sixty plus years in this rural area and had managed not only to eke out a living from the land, but had finally managed to save enough to purchase an additional five acres of land.

He was particularly proud of this new addition to his farm and when an old friend from the state of Texas came into the area and stopped to visit him, he took his friend out to the meadow behind the farm house to show off his newly acquired piece of land. Pointing to an old oak tree a few hundred yards away, he exclaimed. "My new piece of property begins at that tree and runs down to the end of that large meadow, and then south along that stone fence, then back to the edge of that old apple orchard". He beamed with pride as he added, "its a real nice piece of farm land and will make good pasture for my cows".

His old friend from Texas nodded appreciatively and exclaimed in the usual Texas manner. "You know, back home in Texas, I can get in my new pickup truck and drive from sunrise til sunset without ever leaving my property". The old Adirondacker just nodded his head, gave a spat of his tobacco and replied, "You know, Jake, I used to have a truck just like that once". There was no more said as they walked back to the farmhouse and sat down to enjoy a cup of coffee.

AUSABLE

The River talks a language
that only God talks back
Somewhere in those waters
a Spirit dwells
Dark deep currents
rolling silent
through the mountain pass
and white water canyons
roaring with froth and defiance
to the stunned minds
that dare come close to the edge
all sound alike
when asked the great question.

Now, give a simple answer,
"What is the water saying?"
Does anyone know?
It seems that no one knows
Most never hear the question.
It is too hard to listen
to words that mean
more than you can think.
(It's also too hard to love
more than your heart can desire.)

I used to row a wooden boat
with silent tugging strokes
along the wooded banks
in the mists of early dawn
the water breathless still.
I did it so often,
so quietly,

that after a while
I was part of the River;
not a visitor
or an intruder
or a moving object on the surface
but just another aspect
of the River's silent song,
not much different
from the mysterious hungry trout
who were everywhere present
but seldom seen
and only occasionally heard
as they broke the still surface
with random rippled rises.

A TIME FOR EVERYTHING/ AND A TIME TO DOUBT
By Fran Betters

It was the ninth of May back in the mid forties and I went out to look at the large Shad berry bush alongside our driveway in the country. My parents and I lived in a two story house a few miles outside the village of Wilmington and about a half mile from the famous AuSable river. I checked the Shad bush with great care and also with anticipation. With a young lad's impatience with nature, I wanted to see the first blossoms of shads but all I could find were buds that had begun to open. It would be another full twenty four hours before there would be any blossoms on that shad bush. I was disappointed as I walked back to the house and waited for my father to return from his job as a state highway employee. That same Shad tree had blossomed out faithfully for the past three years on the tenth of May but I had hoped that this year, the blossoms would appear a day early. You see, my father was a well known fly fisherman and he proclaimed many times that dry fly fishing begins with the first Shad blossoms and I knew this to be true as "God made little green apples" because my father had told me. I was a young lad in school and the past couple of years, my father and I had walked the half mile through the woods to the river to fish the first evening rise of mayflies on the evening of May tenth, the day those Shad bushes had blossomed and officially opened the first day of fly fishing.

I had desperately hoped that those blossoms would be out and that tonight we would rig up our fly rods and tie on dry flies and make that special walk to the river to catch the first trout of the year on dries. My mother knew what was on my mind and noticed the disappointment on my face when I returned to the house.

I was standing in the driveway in front of our house when the state truck let my father off at the beginning of the long driveway that led past the Shad bush and up to our front porch. I stood and watched as he stopped for a quick look at the Shad tree, silently hoping that a bud had blossomed out since my scrutiny a few minutes earlier. As he walked up the driveway to where I was standing, he shared my concern with the comment "No blossoms yet, uh?" then added, "They'll be out tomorrow". No further comments were made regarding the Shad tree or fly fishing as my father changed from his overalls into a pair of Khaki trousers and we sat down to a home cooked meal my mother had prepared on the Home Comfort wood cook stove. My father ate hurriedly and then pulled out his Walthan pocket watch to observe the time. Looking up at me, he made the one statement that I waited all year to hear. "Well, hurry up and get the fly rods and your reel and net and we'll catch a couple of trout on those royal Wulffs you tied last evening". I gulped down the remainder of the potatoes and cod-fish gravy on my plate and headed for the wood shed where the fly rods were on a shelf above the door. Any other time, my mother would have chastised me for such a rude departure from the table but this was a special evening and she understood the urgency of the occasion. My father and I gathered our gear and headed off through the woods to the river. We had about an hour and a half of fishing time before it would get dark and we would have to head back home.

When we arrived at slant rock pool, we took the silkworm gut leaders from the leader box where they had been soaking and tied them onto the fly lines and then we each took a size ten Royal Wulff and tied it onto the leaders. Soaking the flies in the homemade solution of paraffin and wax that would keep them floating, we selected our respective areas of the stream where we would start fishing. I remember that particular evening well. My father took a nineteen inch brown on the large Wulff just before dark and I caught a thirteen incher. As we walked through the woods the half mile to the house, we discussed the evening fishing. I commented that the trout didn't know the first Shad blossoms were a day away. My father just grinned and taught me another lesson in the ways of nature. He explained that all the truisms were in fact general rules to be followed that would apply well over the years. He then went on to inform me that everyone should keep an open mind and that there are exceptions to every rule. The one comment that has served me well over the years in my pursuit of trout has been his comment that "There is a time when one should doubt all that applies and experiment with new techniques and ideas to be successful".

That one statement "There is a time to doubt all things" is merely another way of telling us to keep an open mind and not be afraid to try something new. It is the common sense approach to every dimension of life and serves as a catalyst to explore, invent and improvise while using those truisms as a base of knowledge to expand our horizons. I have never forgotten the lessons of the Shad tree. It was the beginning of many lessons of life my father taught me.

THE MOST BEAUTIFUL FLOWER

The most beautiful flowers in the world
Are those that bloom from buds of thoughts

OFF THE HOOK
By Fran Betters

The following story was told to me by a local New York State game warden who often stops in my shop along the banks of the AuSable river for a chat and to find out what local fly patterns are producing best.

He was checking the Franklin Falls section of the Saranac river a few years back and saw a gentlemen fishing the flow just below the water falls at the power plant. It was the first part of June and Bass season had not yet opened so he parked his vehicle across the highway and walked down over the bank to where the man was casting. After asking to check his license, he stepped back to the edge of the water and looking down, noticed a stringer with two large bass weighing a good three pounds each. Pulling the stringer nearly out of the water and holding them for observation, he notified the fisherman that bass season was closed and that the bass were illegal. Without a blink or any sign of nervousness, the man exclaimed "I know bass season isn't open yet and I am fishing for Walleyes. These two bass kept hitting my lures and I got tired of them bothering me so I just tied them up. I intended to let them go when I finish fishing". Again without the slightest bit of nervousness or hesitation, the fisherman continued to cast away in a normal manner. The warden was somewhat taken back by this reply and for a minute or two didn't know whether to issue a ticket for illegal taking of bass or to laugh.

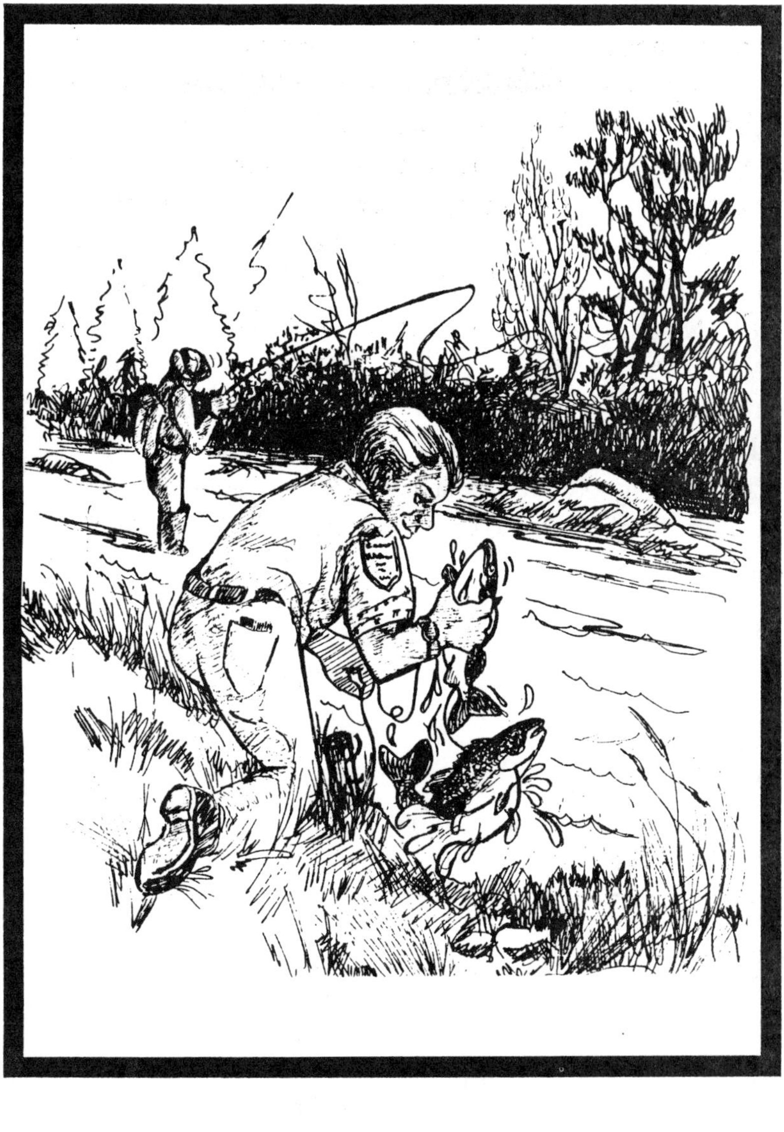

After a moments hesitation, he reached down and pulled up the stringer with the two bass and unhooked them releasing them back into the water where they swam off. He then turned to the fisherman and with stern and authoritative voice answered. "I just let them loose for you, now I think you'd better quit for the day, I don't want you annoying those bass anymore until the season opens". The warden related that it was the best excuse he had ever been given and he felt a reward was in order for coming up with that good of a story. He added however, that he kept a close eye on that local fisherman from then on.

HARVEST TIME FOR BEARS
By Fran Betters

I've always staunchly maintained that if it were possible to pick any set of parents in the world for my own, I would have picked the ones that chose to adopt me at birth. And by the same token, If I could have picked any environment in the world to have lived my childhood, it would have been the one I was injected into.

The small country home where I grew up was like a million other country homes where happy families lived. It had a wooden front porch with a much worn and used swing, the kind that we refer to today as a glider. The kind of a kitchen that brings back fond memories of home baked toll-house cookies and hot bread from the oven, smothered with fresh butter. There was a large living room with an old and large Zenith radio where we always listened to Amos and Andy, Lowell Thomas, Tom Mix, Jack Armstrong, the All American Boy, and of course the Joe Lewis fights.

Just off the kitchen was a woodshed filled with the winter's supply of wood and from the wood shed, a path led led about a hundred feet to a well with a bucket attached to a rope where we got our fresh supply of water every morning and as needed. Just off the living room was a second stairway that led up to the second floor where two bedrooms were located just to the left and to the right of the top hall of the stairway. My room was on the right at the top of the stairs and my mother and father's was at the left at the top of the stairs. There was a window facing the back of the house from my parents bedroom that looked out on the field where two large apple trees were located and in my room the window faced the woods on the West side of the house.

I haven't lived in that old house for over forty years, but if I were blind folded and led back into that house I would be able to find and recognize every single corner and board from the dirt basement beneath the house to the little closets in the bedrooms, and the dark secret places beneath the pantry shelves behind the old kitchen stove where my mother used to put my homemade root beer to "work" alongside the home made beer she made for my father. I remember hearing a bottle explode occasionally when the beer fermented too quickly from the heat in the pantry or because perhaps a little too much sugar might have been added. They say that everything always seems better in retrospect but I can vouch for the fact that both the homemade root beer and the home brew my mother made was far superior to any bought over the counter of your local grocery store today. When it was poured from the bottle, it would have a nice large foamy head on the glass and it had a sparkling and "life" not found in the kind you buy. Just thinking about it now makes me wish I had a bottle of either to drink.

Anyhow, I'm getting away from the story I started to tell, so let me get back on the right track. Just behind our house was our garden where we raised our years supply of beans, potatoes, carrots, cucumbers, spinach and other vegetables that my mother canned every fall and also the tomatoes. In back of the garden about 100 feet from the house were two large apple trees that supplied us with enough apples to make canned apple sauce and fresh home made apple pies in the fall. From the apple trees back to the woods was about another 100 feet and in the right hand corner of the field was our pig pen where we kept our two pigs that we raised each year. And after my father butchered them and scalded them in a barrel of boiling water to remove the bristles we got our supply of ham, pork sausage, blood sausage, head cheese and pig hocks. I can still remember my mother saying that the pig was the most economical animal because you could use everything but the squeal. But during the summer however, when raising them from little piglets to full grown size or butchering weight of about 200 to 250 pounds, they were treated as pets more or less and given names to match their individual pig personalities.

To get on with the story, it was late in November, around the year of my seventh or eight year on the planet and I was awakened

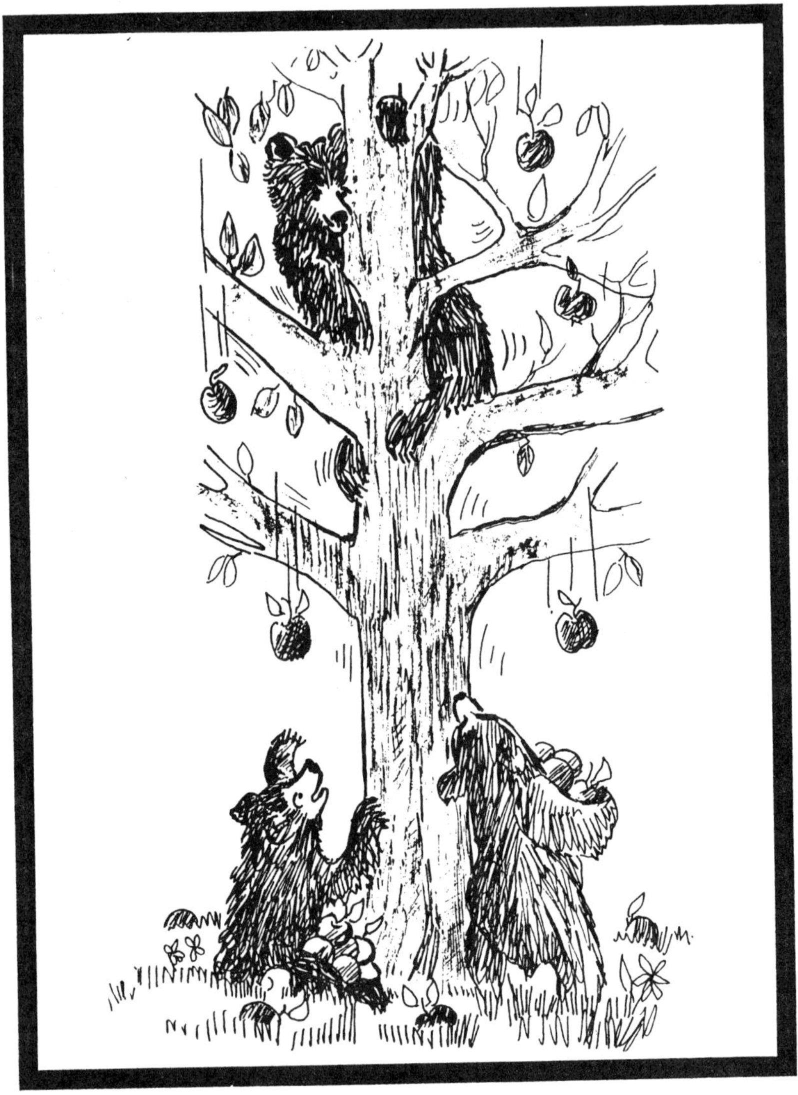

early (right around day break) by my mother and told to come into her bedroom and look out the window. Rubbing my eyes and anxiously climbing out of my nice warm bed, I was ushered into her room to stand in front of the back bedroom window.

In one of the large apple trees behind the house, a large bear was high in the tree shaking it violently in an effort to shake off the remaining apples not harvested. Beneath the tree her two spring cubs were taking the apples and carrying them back into the woods. We watched them as they made about three trips back and forth from the woods to the apple trees. When they returned to the tree for the forth time, they (like children) forgot what mama had told them to do and began playing with each other beneath the trees. This required some chastising so the big bear climbed down from the tree and gave each of her cubs a wallop which sent them rolling on the ground. Each let out a yelp that expressed hurt pride and a promise of better obedience to mama. They immediately went back to the task of gathering apples while mama bear climbed back up into the tree to shake down some more apples. We watched this harvest operation by the bears for about fifteen minutes more, with no more dalliance by the cubs, and then they all left and disappeared back into the woods. We didn't see the bears anymore that fall.

About a week after this episode however we

were awakened in the night by our pigs squealing and making a rumpus. My father grabbed an eight cell flashlight and his 30-30 rifle and went out behind the woodshed and fired a shot into the night air. He commented at the breakfast table that he didn't mind the bear harvesting some of our apples but when it came to our pork, they'd have to pay for it or raise their own. The following week-end, my uncle came over to help with the pig butchering and our supply of pork was secured for the year.

THE SAW THAT NEEDED NEW TEETH
By Fran Betters

*A*s with every industry in the past few decades, the lumbering industry has seen great new technological improvements both in the types of machinery used and in the methods used to harvest the crop of trees and get them to the processing plants or mills. Now, there are the new hydraulic cutters that slice through giant trees in seconds, and large pac-man machines that eat the limbs as fast as they are trimmed from the trees. But perhaps the most radical and progressive piece of equipment in the harvesting of the forest was the invention and introduction of the chain saw. Prior to this, the old fashioned two man crosscut saws were the standard tools of the trade in cutting down the trees and cutting them into sections. It required lots of hard work and sweat and was very time consuming. But as with every new invention, its use and maintenance required the necessary time and knowledge to insure the maximum production time for its use. The chain saw was no exception. This is the story of how one new chain saw was initiated into its role in the harvesting of lumber.

The small community of Tupper Lake (population 7000) is known as a lumber town with a large French Canadian heritage. From the early 1900's, lumbering has been the main industry in that section of the Adirondacks. It was probably at its peak in the forties and fifties.

During this era, the chain saw came into its own and dominated the production of logs from the forest. It was one fall day near the beginning of the lumbering season during this period when one experienced woodsman from north of Montreal, Canada ventured into a lumber camp outside the village of Tupper Lake and applied for a job as a tree faller. He spoke very broken English and when questioned about his experience, could only reply "Me very good worker, me work hard, boss man". Well, this seemed like a most positive attitude for employment so he was hired on the spot. The camp foreman took the new man into the woods on his first day on the job, gave him a new chain saw and pointed out a number of large trees that had been marked for cutting and would later be used as pulp in the paper industry. He also explained that each man was expected to produce in the neighborhood of five cords of pulp wood a day. As he left the new man, the Frenchman was nodding his head vigorously and repeating "Me work hard boss man, me good worker". At the end of the first day, he was the last man to straggle into camp and when the foreman approached him and inquired as to how many cords of pulp he had cut, he was surprised to hear his reply of "One and a half cord, boss man, but me do better tomorrow, me good worker".

    Now the guy seemed to be a most pleasant fellow so the foreman gave him a pat on the back and a word of encouragement saying "You'll break into it, its your first day." The following morning, the new man was up and on the job before any of the other cutters had left the camp and was the last man to return that evening. When once again the foreman approached him and inquired about his day's production, the new man replied "I got almost two cord today, boss man". The third day was a repeat of the second day with about the same production. The foreman could see that the man was very tired and took him by the shoulder and said "Perhaps there is something wrong with your saw, I'll go out with you in the morning and check it out". The foreman had learned that the man had a wife and family back home and needed the work; and being a compassionate man, he wanted to give the new worker every opportunity to produce. To make light of the matter, he said casually "Perhaps your saw needs to see a dentist and get some new teeth". This was a little over the Frenchman's head and his only reply was a toothy grin and the stock "me do better, boss man".

On the fourth morning, the new man was already to leave the camp at first sign of daylight and the foreman accompanied him to the section of woods where he was working. When they arrived, the foreman asked to see the man's saw and when it was handed to him, gave the cord a quick jerk to start the motor. At this, the new lumberjack jumped hastily back away from the saw and quickly putting his hands over his ears, inquired "What dat noise, boss man, what dat noise?". It is needless to say that the new man's production vastly improved after that day of instruction and he became one of the most valuable men in the camp as well as the most congenial.

ONE LAST DIVE
By Fran Betters

*W*ith the Bermuda Triangle not too far off and the ghost of a hundred Spanish vessels groaning beneath the sands around Coffin's Patch, it was hard not to feel a little apprehensive about diving in this area. I'd known a couple of more experienced divers who had come up with pale horror stricken expressions on their faces, taken off their suits and left for shore, never to return to dive again. Well, I'd been in the Bermuda Triangle a number of times without being swallowed up by any supernatural monster beneath the sea and I sure wasn't afraid of some 200 year old pirate sitting in a rotten ship fifty feet or more beneath the sand. If I encountered such an apparition, I'd just ask him for a drink of that 200 year old bottle of rum he most likely would be holding. I took a deep breath, adjusted my regulator and flipped backward over the side of my boat and let myself drift downward through the clear blue water past the sargent majors and blue tangs and other tropical fishes. I finally drifted into a grey murky section of water and downward to my left I could just make out the pinnacle of a high coral column that in the murkiness gave the impression of a remote mountain peak. I shifted my position and kicked off to my right away from the sharp peak. When I looked downward and a little to my right, I noticed another tall column of coral about the same size as the other. I was drifting downward between the two columns and now the pinnacles were above me. It was erie but I couldn't resist the temptation to continue downward. I'd just have to be extra careful.

Suddenly I was in crystal clear water again and the murky layer of water was now above me. Looking down now, I was surprised to see a patch of pure white sand that looked as smooth as glass, but before I had time to marvel at it further, I was standing on the smooth surface. I reached down to scoop up a handful of the fine coral but to my surprise found not the fine texture of coral sand but a smooth marble hard surface so smooth it was almost like it had been polished. Looking ahead of me, I saw two more smaller columns of coral that looked exactly alike. They stood about six feet high, identical to my eye and about four feet apart. My first impression was that someone had placed them this way but I knew that was impossible. As I approached cautiously, I noticed another strange sight. There were two swordfish each about four feet long, one on each side of the opening by the pillars. They were facing each other and their swords were pointing upwards towards each other as if they were guarding the entrance. Neither moved as I approached to within thirty feet of them and stopped. I couldn't believe what I was seeing so I took a deep breath, checked the indicators on my air tanks and sat back on my haunches to try to figure out what this strange sight was all about. A few minutes later I saw a sawfish, also about four feet long come out through the entrance, followed by a four foot long hammerhead shark. In all my years of diving I had never seen these species together. As I watched, the sawfish and hammerhead disappeared around behind the column of coral to my left and I could hear strange noises coming from the other side of the column. I decided to stay put since I knew that if they should both come at me at the same time, one might puncture my air hose.

A few minutes later both the sawfish and hammerhead reappeared from around the coral column, each pushing a long thin slab of coral into the entrance between the two columns, and disappeared inside. The long thin strips of coral appeared to have been cut. My curiosity was aroused to the point where I just had to have a look inside that chamber, but cold chills came over me each time I looked at the two swordfish guarding the entrance. I had to divert their attention somehow so I could get inside.

The thought never crossed my mind that I might be able to go around those pillars but somehow deep inside, I knew for certain that this would not be possible. Although I was not more than thirty feet from those swordfish, they seemed not to see me and paid no attention so I began to inch forward slowly. I had not taken more than two mini steps of a few inches when both fish suddenly turned with their swords facing me. I could feel the hair on the back of my neck stand up and I wanted to turn around, go back up to the top and call it a day, but something was driving me to get inside that chamber.

I looked around to see if I could find anything to throw that might distract them. There was absolutely nothing on the floor. The marble-like slab of polished coral was void of even the tiniest grain of sand. I rechecked my air supply and found one tank to be nearly full. I had another twenty minutes before I would have to start my accent back to the surface. Suddenly I had an idea. Unstrapping the one air tank that was nearly empty, I lay it down on the smooth surface in front of me. I would have to be quick if this were going to work. I quickly unscrewed the valve a half turn and gave the tank a vicious kick with my foot sending it rolling and hissing towards the entrance between the two columns. Air bubbled and hissed from the tank as it rolled toward the entrance. When it was about ten feet away, both swordfish turned and attacked it viciously. I choose this moment to scoot around them and into the entrance and was about ten feet inside before they stopped their assault on the tank and returned to their stations by the pillars. I faced back toward them in anticipation of an attack but they just returned to their original places and assumed their positions. So much for getting in, now I would have to figure out a way to get out, but not before I had a good look around. I shortly wished I had followed my first impulse to go back to my world upstairs. The first thing I noticed was that the entire floor was exactly the same as that outside, a smooth polished coral.

Off to the right there were two sawfish and two hammerheads assembling thin slabs of coral into the shape of coffins, and just beyond, four sand sharks were rubbing their skin vigorously back and forth against the coral coffins to polish them to a glass smooth finish. As they did this, a number of small blowfish were blowing away the dust, all in a very efficient operation. My eyes continued to scan around the large chamber and on my left I noticed two neat rows of coral coffins. Their lids were open and I starred fixedly at the pillows made from bleached sponges, around each of which was wrapped ornate lace coral. On the side of each coffin were highly polished coral name plates. There was one more item that caught my eye. It was a large crate large enough to hold about four of the coffins. The crate was cut roughly from dark coral slabs wound tightly with seaweed.

The whole scene was erie and my knees were trembling and I couldn't get rid of the cold chills that kept creeping up along my spine, and my breath seemed to hang in my throat.

Suddenly the two swordfish at the entrance turned toward me as if on cue, the hammerheads and sawfish turned and slowly began inching their way toward me, their eyes boring into my very soul. At the last second when they were inches away, I panicked and dropped my divers belt and quickly began shooting towards the surface; not caring about nitrogen bubbles or the bends or about anything in this whole world but to get out of that chamber.

When I got to the surface I must have been in a pretty bad state. Another boat picked me up and took me in. I finally recovered but have never been back in the water nor will I ever dive again. When they gave me my divers suit, I found a small polished piece of coral about four inches high and nine inches long and about a quarter inch thick. My name was chiseled perfectly into the coral and below on the left side was the date of my birth. On the right side was the date of my last dive. I have never told this story to anyone before and will vigorously deny it if you tell anyone I told you.

ALL THAT BLOOD
By Fran Betters

*T*his is a story that I remember from my childhood days. My father would often relate it when telling about his days as a lumber camp manager shortly after World Ward One. A large lumber company, called the J. J. Rogers company operated remote lumber camps, and after returning from the war in France in 1919, my father was hired to manage one such camp. He and my mother had just recently been married and at the time my father was hired, my mother was also hired as the camp cook.

The 1920's was a rugged time to be alive and rugged men and women worked a rigid schedule in the remote sections of the Adirondacks, falling, limbing and sectioning the large trees. The trees were then skidded by horse to a log ramp where they rolled with Peeves onto the ramp to await the spring freshets to flood the sluice ways. (large construction troughs) that would float the logs into the rain swollen streams and then downstream to the cutting mills. In those early days, the lumber camps were operated by a majority of French Canadian lumberjacks. One day, one such French Canadian lumberjack found his way to my fathers camp and requested a job. When questioned about his proficiency with an axe, he replied that he was indeed handy with the axe and would do well as a limber. In those days the limbers (these were the men who cut the limbs from the trees after they had been cut down with the large crosscut saws) used double bitted axes and it was critical to keep the axes well sharpened to avoid rebound from the frozen limbs. Many a limber suffered severe cuts when an axe would rebound from a frozen limb and strike them in various parts of the body. The man was hired by my father and put to work in a section about a half mile from the main camp. On the second morning of his job as a limber, the temperature was around zero and the new man was working the trees that had been fallen the previous day. Shortly before noon, the axe he was using rebounded and struck him a glancing blow in the lower leg. He let out a howl of pain and the other men rushed to his side to see how badly he was hurt. One look revealed that the axe had sliced cleanly through the legging and through the heavy wool pants he was wearing. A closer look revealed a profuse amount of red. The man was writhing and groaning and it was obvious he was in great pain. The other men carefully lifted him and carried him the half mile back to the main camp. When they arrived they lay him down on a cot in the main camp and called for my mother to come and take a look. Any woman in a lumber camp hired as a cook most of the time was called on for patching up wounds as well. They carefully cut away the leather legging, and the lower section of the man's pant leg to reveal a pair of bright red flannel long john pajamas. There was a neat slice in the long johns and underneath was a very slight cut, about the size that would be made by a cat scratching him. The amount of blood was about what you'd expect from a cat's scratch. The man was still moaning when they rolled him off the cot onto the floor of the camp and gave him a swift kick in the seat of the pants - telling him to get back to work. It never became quite clear whether the man believed he was badly injured or whether he pulled off his own little joke, but these were the little every day incidents that made life interesting in the lumber camps.

THE WINDOW
By Fran Betters

The following is actually two stories that both originated from the kitchen window of the old farm house I lived in for the first sixteen years of my life. The first story I call "The Boogie Man" and the second is entitled "The Assassin". Both are actual accounts of incidents that took place when I was somewhere between the ages of nine and twelve.

THE BOOGIE MAN
By Fran Betters

It was one of those old fashioned winter nights in the Adirondacks and the old woodstove in the combination kitchen - living room of our old farmhouse was consuming the wood at an alarming rate in an effort to keep the house warm. My father was out there somewhere in the cold standing on the back of a state sanding truck sanding the highways. Sometimes during the night he would make his return to stand his frozen overalls up in the woodshed attached to the kitchen. There they would thaw and then be brought in to dry behind the stove. He would put on a fresh pair and grab another pair of liners for his buckskin mittens and return to the back of the sand truck to finish the nights work. It was about six thirty this particular evening and my mother was sitting in an old rocker listening to Amos and Andy on the tube radio and not paying much attention to me since I was engrossed in the latest issue of the Captain Marvel comic book. I sat by the kitchen window and was ever aware of the howling wind and snow blowing outside against the panes of glass but I was cozy and secure inside. It was Friday evening and if the storm stopped, my dad would be off sometime tomorrow and after catching up on his much needed sleep, he might take me with him into the woods and I'd watch while he and our neighbor, Mr. Tanton, loaded wood on the sleigh, and maybe they would let me ride while the horse pulled the load of wood back down behind the woodshed where it would be later sawed and split and then piled to dry for next winter's supply. These were the thoughts of a happy nine or ten year old in a well balanced environment. The comic book was nearly finished and the excitement of Captain Marvel's last escapade had made me a little hungry. I laid the comic book aside and went into the pantry, and taking a small can of tomatoes from the shelf, opened it and then sprinkled a spoon of sugar over them. Tomatoes with a liberal sprinkling of sugar was one of my favorite childhood snacks. My mother was still seated in the opposite corner of the large room when I returned to my seat at the table and sat down next to the window. The wind was still howling and the snow seemed to be blowing even harder. It was not the kind of night that anyone wanted to be outside in and I thought of my father out there and worried that he would be cold.

My mother was engrossed in the act of knitting a pair of mittens for me and hadn't seen me sit down with the dish of tomatoes and sugar. I took a spoonful of the tomatoes, ate them and had just put the second spoonful in my mouth when I turned toward the window. A grotesque face was pressed against the window pane and two frost encrusted hands framed the face flat against the window pane. I let out a scream and the mouthful of tomatoes went flying outward into the air and onto the table. My mother looked up at the effusion of red from my mouth and immediately thought it was blood. She let out a scream "What's wrong with you" and rushed to my side to grab me. Finally realizing that what she saw was tomatoes and not blood, she looked towards the window which I was gesturing towards. But by this time, there was no one there. My father had entered from the woodshed and walked on in through the kitchen door with a sheepish expression on his face. He had plastered his frost covered face and mittens against the window pane to scare me as I sat there and to say that he had succeeded was the understatement of the year. He said he hadn't meant to scare us to death but my poor mother must have had a near heart attack from seeing that huge mouthful of tomatoes flying all over the table. We all had a good laugh after our hearts stopped racing but my father never attempted to scare me again in that manner. It was the last time the Boogie Man appeared at my kitchen window.

engrossed in the latest issue of the Captain Marvel comic book. I sat by the kitchen window and was ever aware of the howling wind and snow blowing outside against the panes of glass but I was cozy and secure inside. It was Friday evening and if the storm stopped, my dad would be off sometime tomorrow and after catching up on his much needed sleep, he might take me with him into the woods and I'd watch while he and our neighbor, Mr. Tanton, loaded wood on the sleigh, and maybe they would let me ride while the horse pulled the load of wood back down behind the woodshed where it would be later sawed and split and then piled to dry for next winter's supply. These were the thoughts of a happy nine or ten year old in a well balanced environment. The comic book was nearly finished and the excitement of Captain Marvel's last escapade had made me a little hungry. I laid the comic book aside and went into the pantry, and taking a small can of tomatoes from the shelf, opened it and then sprinkled a spoon of sugar over them. Tomatoes with a liberal sprinkling of sugar was one of my favorite childhood snacks. My mother was still seated in the opposite corner of the large room when I returned to my seat at the table and sat down next to the window. The wind was still howling and the snow seemed to be blowing even harder. It was not the kind of night that anyone wanted to be outside in and I thought of my father out there and worried that he would be cold.

My mother was engrossed in the act of knitting a pair of mittens for me and hadn't seen me sit down with the dish of tomatoes and sugar. I took a spoonful of the tomatoes, ate them and had just put the second spoonful in my mouth when I turned toward the window. A grotesque face was pressed against the window pane and two frost encrusted hands framed the face flat against the window pane. I let out a scream and the mouthful of tomatoes went flying outward into the air and onto the table. My mother looked up at the effusion of red from my mouth and immediately thought it was blood. She let out a scream "What's wrong with you" and rushed to my side to grab me. Finally realizing that what she saw was tomatoes and not blood, she looked towards the window which I was gesturing towards. But by this time, there was no one there. My father had entered from the woodshed and walked on in through the kitchen door with a sheepish expression on his face. He had plastered his frost covered face and mittens against the window pane to scare me as I sat there and to say that he had succeeded was the understatement of the year. He said he hadn't meant to scare us to death but my poor mother must have had a near heart attack from seeing that huge mouthful of tomatoes flying all over the table. We all had a good laugh after our hearts stopped racing but my father never attempted to scare me again in that manner. It was the last time the Boogie Man appeared at my kitchen window.

THE ASSASSIN
By Fran Betters

A couple of years later, that same window was to play another memorable incident in my life. Our closest neighbor lived about a half mile from our house, and Alvin, their youngest son also happened to be my best friend. We skied the old logging trails together, rode his father's horses and even had friendly competitions to see who could chop the most firewood in the same amount of time. When we were each about eleven, our fathers bought us each a Ryder pump BB gun and from that very day until we became old enough to have real rifles, every nickel and dime we earned from our parents was spent on BBs for our war games, and the wildwest battles with each other. We both became good shots and we made a solemn agreement never to aim at each other's head. Arms and legs were fair game and our guns were pumped at low power so as not to sting too much when they hit. Once I caught a BB in the palm of my hand as I reached up to grab a rafter above my head in an old barn I was hiding in. We had to dig it out from under the skin with a small pen knife and I had a sore hand for a few days but I never told my mother what had happened. It would have meant us having the guns taken away from us.

One November afternoon just before darkness fell, I was standing at the sink in our kitchen washing up for dinner and my mother was cooking the dinner on the old wood stove. I had just finished wiping my hands when there came a crash of glass from the window and the sound of a shot. At the same time I felt something hit me in the lower leg and I let out a whelp and like a wounded soldier is supposed to do when shot, I fell to the floor. During this sequence of action, my mother let out a scream and again rushed to my side, at the same time glancing toward the window to see what had happened. What she saw was Alvin running away at a dead run back to the neck of woods that led to the large open field he would have to cross before reaching his home. In his panic he dropped his trusty weapon outside the window. When he had aimed at me through the window, in the excitement of the battle, he had accidentally pulled the trigger and the BB gun had gone off. His aim had been true but it had scared the hell out of the window, my mother and me and it surprised Alvin most of all. My mother went outside and picked up the BB gun and brought it in the house and leaned it up against the wall in the corner. That evening my father replaced the panel of glass in the window and the next day we waited for Alvin to come over. He hadn't shown up by noon so my mother told me to take his BB gun over to him and tell him not to worry, she wasn't going to tell his mother or father what had happened. And that she knew he hadn't meant to shoot through the window. It was years later that my mother mentioned the incident to his folks and everyone had a good laugh. The assassin never struck again.

THE GREAT GOOSE FARMING OPERATION
By Fran Betters

*S*ome years ago when I was a young lad living in the rural area of the adirondacks, I occasionally recall two older gentlemen who farmed about a half mile from our home. They didn't do much in the way of farming, they had only two cows, a few chickens, a horse and strangely, a mule. It was the only one I ever remember seeing during my entire childhood years. They planted a sufficient amount of potatoes and vegetables to sustain themselves, and like so many other small farmers in those days, just managed to make ends meet. What little money was needed to buy staples, chewing tobacco etc. was obtained by selling fire wood, eggs or by trading whatever they had to a neighbor for something they didn't have. When work was available, it was usually on a part-time basis, or working a few days doing odd jobs such as cutting ice blocks in the winter to put up for the summer ice supply.

Now Mr. Zebra, that was the name of the older of the two gentlemen. I remember his name because a few years later, he was kicked in the head by the mule and died shortly after. Well, anyway, Mr. Zebra and his partner took a trip over to a small town on the other side of Whiteface mountain, called Vermontville and while they were there, they saw another farmer with a gaggle of geese. The bought a dozen of the goose eggs to take home and then one or the other, or perhaps both, got the idea that raising geese would be the up and coming thing to do. The final decision took them about two weeks of hard thinking after they had returned home to their little cabin. But after much thought, they decided to make the big move.

One of them got out an old Sears and Roebuck catalogue and thumbed through it until they saw a picture of a goose. One of them could do a little writing but not very much. It took awhile but finally they got the catalog number of the goose down on an order form and were about to seal it when the other remarked that he didn't think they could do much with one goose and had probably better order another one if they planned on raising any. This led to a much larger problem since after much discussion, they couldn't decide whether the plural of goose was gooses, geese, or geeses. They didn't want to appear stupid so Mr. Zebra, he was the smarter of the two, at least until he got kicked in the head by the mule and died. Well, he just sat back down at the table and wrote at the bottom of the order form. P.S. "Please send us another"

It must have worked because about three weeks later, they received their pair of geese. The goose farming business was not a success however, as one of the geese died a couple of weeks later. The remaining goose became a good pet and lived with them inside their little cabin for three years. It died shortly before Mr. Zebra was kicked in the head by their mule.

THE BELLIGERANT BULL
By Fran Betters

As fall and the coming hunting season approaches it always brings to mind a bow hunting trip in the Catskills that took place a few years ago.

It was a beautiful cool crisp fall day and the bow season had opened the previous day in the area where our group would be hunting. We had all met at the home of my good friend, Jack Smith, and his wife Gert had cooked us a hearty breakfast of bacon and eggs to get us started for the day. Joining us in the hunting party was his brother Doug and our good friend, Keith Roberts. We'd all had experience hunting with the bow and arrow so it was no new adventure but as always, the thrill and expectation of the hunts was always there and we all looked forward to another pleasant day in the woods, and hopefully an exciting day of adventure. As it turned out, it proved to be a little more adventurous and exciting than I had hoped.

My friend's home was located in the little town of Palenville alongside the Katterskill Creek and a short distance from where Rip Van Winkle took his extended nap. We left his house just prior to daylight and started the trip up the mountain to Hanes Falls, hence to the town of Hunter and then cut across on a dirt road to Jewett Center to hunt an area we called "The

Romper Room". It was a beautiful little section of woods and most of the time we hunted there, we saw some deer.

We made a number of small hunts in the area without anyone getting a good shot at a deer although we did see deer. We were all experienced enough in bow hunting so that unless we had what we considered a good shot and a good chance of killing the deer, we abstained from taking luck shots or shots at very long distances.

After a lunch at a nearby diner about one, we decided to go over to the other side of the mountain to try our luck there. The area we choose to hunt bordered on a small creek and consisted of a number of patches of woods that bordered on one side of a large pasture that a farmer had fenced off, where his cattle could feed.

Separating to cover a larger area, we each cautiously hunted our way along the orchards and woods hoping to get a shot at a deer or else chase one out to another of our party.

It was a couple of hours later when Doug and Jack returned to where I was hunting and Doug exclaimed that he had wounded a deer quite bad and lost track of it so we would have to scour the area in hopes of finding the deer. He was quite emphatic in the fact that the deer was hit hard and would not go far but since there was no snow on the ground and an arrow stuck in a deer doesn't always produce a lot of blood, it might be a job locating the deer.

Each of us started off again in a different direction with a different guess on just where the deer might have gone to lie down and die or recover from its wounds - as the case might be. Jack elected to cross the small creek and search up along side while Doug stayed on the side we were already on, while I elected to wander away from the creek to the patches of woods and meadowland a few hundred yards from the creek.

I had zig-zagged through patches of woods and tall grass for a half hour when I came to the barbed wire fence that enclosed the large pasture. Inside the pasture, I noticed more small patches of woods and sections of tall grass with little valleys and hills that might serve as good hiding places for a wounded deer.

Standing my bow against the fencepost, I rolled beneath the fence and stood up on the other side reclaiming my bow before heading off into the pasture to search the more promising areas where a deer might hide.

I had covered a quite large area that included a number of patches of woods and tall grass when I noticed in the immediate distance an indentation in the ground that seemed to be a hole that was grown over with grass and mounds of dirt - also grass covered, around it. Perhaps it was a spot where the farmer had buried a horse some time ago and the ground had sunken in and new grass had grown to cover the spot. Anyway, I started toward the area and when I got to the higher region around the indented area, I looked down and saw the deer lying there on its side. I quickly notched an arrow with the idea of getting a good shot to put the deer out of its misery but there was no need. A minute of quiet observation told me that the deer was dead. I was about to start back across the pasture to find the rest of the guys and tell them that I had located the deer when I heard a galloping thumping sound that seemed to be getting closer. I turned to see - much to my dismay I might add, a large bull with it's head down and coming to claim the spot where I was standing.

Needless to say, I was not at all happy about my predicament and for a moment, I didn't know whether to arm myself with the bow and arrow or try to get away from the charging bull. The indented ground where the deer was lying offered no adequate protection and the thought of explaining why I had shot an arrow into a farmer's bull seemed a greater hazard then the bull that was quickly gaining ground. As the distance quickly decreased between us, I made the decision not to put an arrow in the bow and instead grabbed the bow by one end and swung it in a wide loop, hollering as loud as I could, hoping to scare the bull off. My heart was in my throat as the bull turned a few feet before reaching me and veered off across the pasture. Watching the bull as he made a wide circle and started back toward me. I backed slowly toward the fence in the distance. Holding the bow above my head, I was again ready to swing it when he made his second pass at me. He came within a dozen feet of me again before veering off as I continued my journey across the wide expanse of pasture that seemed a hundred miles away. This scene was repeated about a dozen times and it seemed like an eternity before I reached the fence and rolled under it to the safety of the other side.

After the bull made his last charge, he just stood there staring at me and I hoped with all my heart that he wouldn't come charging across the fence that seemed to be little more than a token barrier to an animal his size.

We continued to stare at each other for a few minutes and it seemed almost as if he was laughing at me and daring me to come back so he could play with me some more. I was more than happy that the game was over.

A few minutes later I was joined by Doug, Jack and Keith and they laughed when I told them about my close call with the belligerant bull. Keith laughed the hardest of all of us as he told us about the bull and that it was just playing and wouldn't hurt us. I believed him after he went under the fence and walked toward the bull, but just to make sure, I waited until both Jack and Doug made their entry into the pasture before joining them. I kept my eyes closely on the bull as we made our way over to where the deer was lying and I swear I could see a gleam in that animals eyes as he eyed me and pranced around us. I've always thought that a little bull goes a long ways and this was just a little too much bull for me to swallow. I like my hunting trips to be a little more on the peaceful side.

The Gift
By Fran Betters

Special moments from the past
Or friends that have long gone
Leave naught but pleasant memories
Like the lyrics of a song

Those moments we cannot relive
Old friends we can't replace
But memories they leave behind
Even time cannot erase

Each year we live, another leaf
Is taken from the tree
But each friend that goes
Will leave for me, another memory

THE NIGHTTIME INTRUDER
By Fran Betters

The trail up the mountain was well marked and Roy and Becky had covered nearly two miles by ten o'clock. They had stopped around eight thirty and purchased a nylon two man tent and a small propane camp stove and groceries that were now wrapped safely in the sleeping bag that was folded inside Roy's small back pack. By the time they had started the climb up the mountain, it had been a few minutes after nine. It was eight miles to the top and at a leisurely pace, they could make it easily by two in the afternoon. They planned on spending the night together on top of the mountain and then having a nice breakfast of bacon and eggs, and then coming back down the mountain. They had promised both their parents they would be back the next evening. Roy and Becky could both smell the bacon in the pack. For supper that evening they had brought along some freeze dried chicken noodle soup, a small bottle of water and a pound of hamburger, along with a package of freeze dried scalloped potatoes. Roy and Becky had been married only two weeks and this was their first camping trip together as husband and wife.

By eleven o'clock, they had made another two miles and the warm autumn sun made occasional appearances through the clouds on the beautiful autumn day. The forecast had been for a clear cool night and they were looking forward to a night under the stars on the mountain, wrapped cozily in each other's arms inside their double sleeping bag inside their little tent.

 Where the trail was wide enough, they walked beside each other holding hands, occasionally stopping to gaze down into a ravine to watch squirrels playing in the dry leaves. Once they caught sight of a red fox in the distance. It was only five of two when they made it to the top and picked a good spot about a hundred feet back to put up their little tent. They spent the next couple of hours gathering dry sticks to build a little fire and sat on the ledge looking out over the mountainside enjoying the scenery. Just before darkness fell, they built a little fire holding area from stones and made a little fire before lighting the small propane stove. Becky made the soup and put the hamburgers in the small fold-up frying pan from the pack and set it on the small compact burner of the propane stove to cook. The night air had dropped the temperature down to around twenty degrees and they huddled around the campfire to stay warm as they enjoyed the soup first and then the hamburger and scalloped potatoes. Afterwards, they used a little water from the water bottle to wipe out the pan and the plastic bowl. Then wrapping it in paper towels, they placed it back in the pack to be ready for breakfast. Roy dug a small hole in the ground and buried the paper plates they had eaten on and the dirty paper towels used to wipe their hands and to wipe out the pan and bowl. It was about six thirty when they decided to crawl into the double sleeping bag.

Taking off their clothes, they slid into the bag together and locked their arms around each other to get warm.

Making love inside the double sleeping bag was a first time experience for them and about an hour later, they fell asleep in each others arms, alone together on the mountain beneath a star laden sky. Once during the night Becky awoke and gazed wondrously up to look at the handle of the big dipper seen through the small opening in the tent.

She was the first to awaken just as the first rays of dawn penetrated the tent. During the night, she had turned and her back was pressed against her husbands chest and one arm was curled around her with his hand cupped around her breast. She opened her eyes sleepily for a moment, she thought she was dreaming. Starring directly into her face only inches away was a masked face. She closed her eyes and opened them for a second time to make sure it wasn't a dream. She started to scream but no sound came out of her mouth. She starred at the face as it stared back at her without a sound. She slowly slid her hand back groping for her husbands hand to awaken him. She dug her nails into his hand and he stirred beside her and his head pressed against her neck as he opened his eyes and looked over at the masked face still staring back at them. Then they both started to laugh. Curled up beside them against the sleeping bag was a large mother coon. She had come into the tent during the night and curled up against the sleeping bag to get out of the cold.

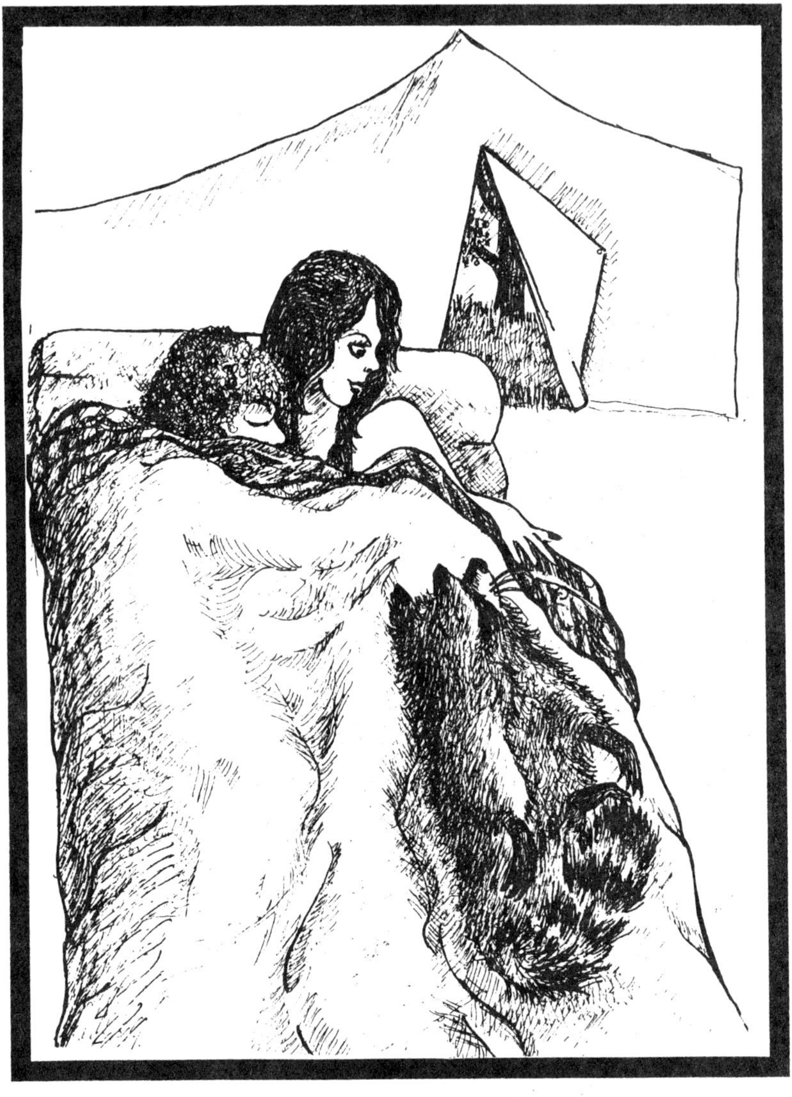

When they moved, the mother coon slowly arose from her resting place and waddled out through the tent fly and into the woods. Roy and Becky discovered a few minutes later, after climbing out of the bag and getting dressed that the coon had eaten their bacon they had foolishly left out on the stones of the fireplace. Four of the six eggs they had brought were also gone. But mother coon had thoughtfully left two for their breakfast.

They made instant coffee with the remaining water in the water bottle and fried the two eggs. They then sat for awhile on the ledges looking out over the mountain side and held hands for a long while before disassembling their tent and packing it inside the back pack before starting the hike back down the mountain. They gladly traded the breakfast they had missed for the memory of that evening that they would recall often over the next fifty years of marriage. Making the same climb up the mountain would happen many times over the years but they never had the privilege of sharing their sleeping bag with mother coon again.

*T*he following poem is dedicated to the memory of my good friend Clyde Ames who often recited this poem at the gathering of friends. I once had him recite it to a prison warden who was visiting one evening without telling him what the man's job was until after the recitation. It provided us with another good laugh.

CHRISTMAS IN THE PRISON

I was Christmas in the prison
and the convicts were all there
seated round the table
reading convict's bill of fare

When in walked the warden
and he said to them all
"Merry Christmas, all you convicts"
and the convicts answered "Balls"

This made the warden angry
and he swore by all the Gods
"You shall have no Christmas pudding,
you dirty low down dogs".

When up jumped a burly convict
with a voice as hard as brass
"We don't want your Christmas pudding
you can shove it up your

MY FRIEND - THE ROBIN
By Fran Betters

My bedroom window faces East and when the first rays of sun peek up over the horizon, they shine in at an angle to light touch me awake. Two weeks ago, before the sun put its first rays of light over the horizon, A strange sound nudged me from my sound sleep. As I opened my eyes and tried to put some recognition into the strange flapping sound, it repeated itself perhaps a half dozen times and finally through the dim light of early dawn, I was able to pin point the sound as coming from the window and slowly recognized the shape of a large bird that was persistently trying to get into my bedroom.

I lie there watching the bird as he would alternately peck at the window and then flap its wings. As the daylight rapidly provided a better view, I saw that it was a large Robin.

The Robin would sit there looking intently around inside and then make another attempt to enter through the window.

After arising and dressing I walked to the window where the bird was still sitting and the bird flew to a tree a dozen feet from the window ledge and proceeded to watch me. After a minute or two, the bird then returned to the window sill and looked intently at me, moving it's head from side to side as if inspecting me to determine what sort of strange creature I might be.

Having a fondness for all animals and birds alike, I discussed the weather and made a remark about what a remarkable bird it was and then went about my daily living. A couple of hours later, when going back into my bedroom for something, I noted that the bird was still there sitting on the window sill with the same determined curiosity. This strange behavior by the Robin (A large female incidentally) has been a daily occurrence for more than two weeks now except that there has been a further development. Mrs. Robin has since built a large nest on the corner window sill of an adjacent window.

When she is not sitting on the nest containing four newly deposited Robin's eggs, she keeps her vigil on my window sill and continues to inspect the interior of my bedroom with the utmost scrutiny.

Mrs. Robin has become a welcomed friend and I continue to make casual comments to the bird each morning or when ever I enter my bedroom. The Robin seems to have a distinct inquisitive personality and we have developed a friendship. At time now when I walk over to the bedroom window where she is sitting, she will remain instead of flying off to perch on the nearby tree, indicating a trust that was not given two weeks ago.

The other day I decided to test the bird's intellectual capacity to determine if Mrs. Robin might have a fondness for poetry. I recited the following poem to the bird and I think I detected a sardonic smile on the bird's face, as if to indicate she knew that I was only kidding.

THE ROBIN

As I awoke this morning
With all, things bright and gay
A Robin perched upon my sill
To signal coming day

The Robin's voice was sweet and gay
And softly did it sing
And thoughts of happiness and joy
Into my heart did spring

And as I sat there by my window
And I paused, a moments lull
I gently closed the window
And crushed the Robin's skull.

THE ADVENTUROUS CHIPMUNKS
By Fran Betters

Some years back, I had a friend who was quite keen on early Morning fly fishing and she would often awaken me about five O'clock in the morning by calling my name beneath my bedroom window to get me up and go fishing with her.

Many a morning we spent together along the banks of our favorite trout stream or fishing from a canoe above the impoundment at Wilmington on the AuSable river.

Many lessons regarding the nature of animals were learned on the waters of the stream as we shared these many happy hours together. One incident that stands out in my memory best involved a pair of Chipmunks.

We had left my home about five in the morning of that particular day and had taken my small canoe and paddled the two miles upstream from the Wilmington dam to the headwaters of the impoundment. After beaching the canoe on a sandbar, we put our fly fishing gear together and proceeded to wade upstream to a large pool below an island where we would start fishing.

It was a beautiful June morning and the first rays of sunshine was just beginning to peak over the tree tops, and many tiny insects were starting to hatch out from among the bushes along the stream bank. Everything pointed to a morning of fine trout fishing and we were not to be disappointed.

The heavy currents from each side of the island joined together in a vortex just downstream of the island and just left of center below this, there was a large rock that we waded to so we would be able to cast to the currents coming from either side and to the heavy run in the middle of the stream. Standing beside each other, we were able to cover the entire pool with our casts as well as the currents that washed food into the pool from either side of the stream.

We fished in this fashion for about a half hour and each of us took a couple of nice trout - returning them to the stream.

About a hundred yards upstream was another large pool and we decided to wade up into the fast water and fish that section for a while. There was a number of converging currents coming into the pool and a very large boulder on the left bank of the stream. Wading to the center of the stream, we positioned ourselves to cast to the better sections of the pool and took a few minutes to enjoy the beauty that surrounded us. There were wild rose bushes along the bank and the sweet fragrance of the petals drifted out to where we were standing.

We were taking it all in when my companion nudged me and quietly whispered "Look - there on the rock" pointing to the top of the large boulder where two full grown chipmunks had just appeared. They were only inches apart and were looking down at the river as if they were contemplating a swim across the stream. As we watched, she whispered those exact sentiments "it looks like they are going to jump in". No sooner were the words away from her lips when they both simultaneously dived into the water and began to swim across to the other side of the stream. Staying close together, they did what we humans call the dog paddle with their little feet paddling furiously while they held their heads and tails high in an attempt to keep them dry. Each time they came to some heavier current, it would begin to wash them downstream a number of feet but as soon as they entered a quieter section of the stream, they again made progress up and across. We watched them with our complete attention for nearly ten minutes until they finally made it to the bank on the opposite side of the stream directly across from where they had made their plunge.

We continued to watch us as they scampered up onto the grassy bank and shook water from their little bodies and disappeared into the woods. It once again verified the tenacity and perseverance that most animals seem to possess. If two little chipmunks dared to attempt the crossing of such a rugged stream with the conviction and confidence that they could make it to the other side, what might we human creatures accomplish if only we dared to take that same approach to life in everything we set out to do.

MY FREIEND HERMAN
By Fran Betters

We humans, at least most of us, have always seemed to have a slightly contemptuous superiority towards any creature that didn't speak our own language. Perhaps it is a psychological boost to our ego to regard all creatures we can't communicate with as inferior. There are many times when I question the wisdom of this practice.

I've always had a fond regard for all animals (especially those not disposed to add me to their diet) and this attitude has allowed me many insights into the animal world and made me very aware of just how much there is to be learned by shucking off this superior attitude of man and treating animals as equals. I've been surprised to find that quite often animals have in turn given me the same respect and benefit of doubt. The following is a story about a good friend, companion and sometime confident for about fifteen years.

His name was Herman and all my friends who knew Herman thought him to be quite a character and regarded him with a great deal of affection. Herman admittedly had a somewhat superior attitude but his temperament was always friendly and easygoing and if anyone ever showed the slightest antagonism or dislike (which was very rare), Herman would just walk away as if to say "I've got more important things to do than waste my time on ignorant people.

You see, I knew Herman for a couple of years myself before I discovered that he was of superior intelligence and that he was different - so to speak. I knew of course that Herman was a CAT but it took me quite a while to realize that he was unlike most other cats I had meet during my lifetime. Oh, he possessed all the unique qualities that cats are supposed to have; independence, self sufficiency, agility, patience, a natural instinct for danger and an insatiable curiosity, but he epitomized each particular quality to an art where it was under his complete control at all times. In addition, Herman also possessed qualities not usually associated with feline behavior and these qualities often surprised friends and even myself at times. For example, though he was as independent as any cat could be, he would always condescend to come over to you when asked in a civil manner; and when asked not to do a particular act that might be annoying to someone, would almost always comply. Sometimes this compliance would be accompanied by a look of disdain so as to let the person who requested the favor know he wasn't particularly happy about doing it, but if this was the way they felt, he'd go along with it.

Herman would exemplify the virtue of patience by sitting for a couple of hours in front of the TV watching a program, even if it were one he didn't think was very interesting. However, his patience towards a child or adult who treated him more as an object was somewhat more limited. He would allow anyone to pick him up in any manner whatsoever, even upside down by the legs, and hold him for a limit of about three minutes. Then he would gently but with a magical dexterity, extricate himself from such an absurd position and find a place where the "stupid humanoid creature who didn't know the difference between a rag doll and a cat" could not get to him. He always seemed to take great care never to offend anyone and I never once knew Herman to scratch or bite anyone, under even the most extenuating circumstances. In fact, as I came to regard Herman as a respected member of the family, there were times when I felt like coming to his defence by scratching or biting some inconsiderate brat that was trying to pick him up by the tail or by the ears, but each time before I could intervene, Herman somehow managed to escape in the most diplomatic manner.

Herman had his specific likes and dislikes and at times could be quite cat-headed about them. For instance, he was especially fond of people and doted on attention given him by the many customers that came into my sports shop. He would sit for hours on the glass counter next to my fly tying desk and watch me tie flies, accepting a gentle stroke or kind word from the customers as they came and went. If he became too bored with this after a while, he would leave his usual position there and go over and climb into a glass showcase where the fishing creels were displayed. He would position himself behind the glass where he would be protected from probing hands and here, he would settle down and take a nap for an hour or two. Many of the customers often mistook him for a stuffed cat during these siesta periods.

Herman's biggest dislike was of snow and cold weather. His journeys out of doors during the winter months to go to the bathroom were very brief and when he returned to the door, his voice left no doubt that he would immediately like to be let back in. Once inside, if the time spent outside had been for any duration, he would go over and stand next to the electric wall heater until his body returned to room temperature again. His favorite winter program during the colder months was Hawaii 5-0. I think he just enjoyed looking at those warm beaches and all that sand.

Herman's preference for a particular brand of cat food was to eventually get him in trouble. Like most other cats, he liked fish, an occasional bowl of milk and some types of people food but once he discovered Tender Vittles, there was nothing else, including fish, that would satisfy his taste buds as well. Each time I came back from a shopping trip, he would stand while I unpacked the groceries until he spotted the boxes of Tender Vittles, then a contented expression would appear on his face, knowing that we had stocked in another weeks supply of his favorite food. He quickly learned how to climb up onto the pantry shelf and knock down the box of Tender Vittles. Then he would open and take out one or more of the aluminum foil packets, tear them open and have his own little feast while I was out of the house. The effort to deceive him by removing all the packets from the Tender Vittles box and putting them inside another box was, needless to say, in vain. He could spot the correct box immediately and only when the packets were stored securely away in a metal cookie tin, was he stymied.

When Herman was about nine years old, his passion for Tender Vittles and his refusal to eat anything else created a problem. He developed a skin rash and began to lose much of his hair. A few trips to the Vet's office and the cause was diagnosed as a vitamin deficiency or some such problem with his diet and it was decided that he would have to change his diet. In addition, we were given a powder to be mixed with water and he was to receive a bath in this solution once a day for a week or two. This treatment was needless to say, not to Herman's liking. A friend who was very fond of Herman volunteered to give him his daily bath, Herman would not fight or scratch as this was beneath his dignity, but each time she immersed him in the large metal tub and gave him a good lathering in his special bath solution, Herman would howl with the most forlorn expression of pain and wounded dignity -

so that neighbors two miles away reported banshees in the area.

During the weeks it took for Herman's hair to grow back, he spent a great deal of time standing over or next to the wall heater to stay warm. The occasional times that he would walk into the front of the large full length mirror in the bathroom, would bring a pained expression to his face as he surveyed himself - sans hair. It was clear his vanity was gravely wounded and during this period, he kept more to himself, avoiding both friends and visitors alike. When his hair finally became full again, he once again returned to his social commitments. These were indeed a rough two or three months for Herman and the transition period where he had to cut back on his favorite food was not at all a happy period for him.

During Herman's first formative year from kitten to cathood, he spent much of his time exploring the large house and the sport shop that was to be his home for the fifteen years that he lived. He learned quickly how to slide the closet doors open leading from my large living room into the guest bedroom. When he didn't want to be disturbed, he would slide open the closet door and go in and get up on the bed and take a nap. This practice led to some interesting moments as well as funny ones.

Once a friend was visiting me and as we sat in the kitchen bar counter having a couple of beers and discussing fishing conditions and other earth shaking problems, my friend happened to notice the closet door opening slowly behind the TV set. He made a vague comment about ghosts in the house, doors opening etc. He of course didn't know that Herman had just finished taking his nap and had come out of the bedroom through the closet and into the living room. The large floor model TV hid Herman from his view. I ignored the remark and a couple of beers later when my friend had gone to the refrigerator to retrieve two fresh ones, I picked up Herman off the couch where he had migrated and too him back into the guest bedroom and closed the door. At the same time I quietly pushed the closet door closed and returned to the kitchen as my friend opened the two fresh beers. I knew it would only be a matter of minutes before Herman again exited the bedroom via the closet door, as I made a comment about doors mysteriously opening - with just enough innuendo without being obvious. This of course focused his attention once more on the closet door and right on cue, Herman made his entry via the closet door back into the living room completely hidden behind the large TV and then back around to his spot on the living room couch out of sight.

My friend finished his beer after mumbling something more about the house being haunted and quickly left - while throwing a furtive sidelong glance toward the closet. It was not until some time later on another visit that I pointed out Herman's knack of opening doors. I think it was also about this time that my friend informed me I was an illegitimate child.

By the time Herman had grown to be a full sized cat, he had explored every inch of the house and the shop and he considered both properties and the surrounding acreage his domain. It was therefore probably very much a surprise when at the age of two, he awoke one day from a nap in the guest bedroom, exited into the living room and found another strange four legged creature boogying around on the living room carpet. A friend had given me a ten week old Labrador puppy which I promptly named Smokey in deference to the smoke colored ball of fur surrounding the energized dynamo inside. Herman's first response upon seeing Smokey was to stop and stare with a queer concern on his face that translated into "I hope what ever you are, you're only visiting". Smokey's reaction was to freeze from the playful prances and for a full moment they faced each other down. When Herman made the first move towards the puppy, Smokey quickly accelerated to a full gallop and with a life saving leap, landed on my lap and began to cry in fear of this strange yellow animal that was about to attack. This of course, was Herman's written in blood proof that he controlled the premises and he never forgot it - even after Smokey had outgrown him by some forty pounds.

It was the beginning of a beautiful

friendship between the two and rarely a day went by that they didn't spend an hour thinking up new games and tricks to play on each other. One of Herman's favorites was to come up behind the couch when the dog was sleeping on the floor in front of the couch. Herman would then leap onto the back of the couch and then jump off landing on the unsuspecting dog. This would be followed by ten or fifteen minutes of frantic play action while they rolled and raced around the living room, often with Herman's head held firmly but gently in Smokey's mouth while the cat held on for dear life with both feet around the dog's neck. They never once hurt each other and it was nearly always Herman who decided the allotted time for playing was up and it was time to get back to the serious business of sleeping or eating.

On those rare occasions that Herman found himself in distress, Smokey was on hand to protect him or to lend a sympathetic ear. When Herman was going through the bad times with the daily baths, Smokey exhibited much concern over Herman's painful distress howls and I am sure that had anyone tried to do Herman harm, Smokey would have taken proper steps to defend him.

Herman once took a trip without ever being aware of it. Once while working on a set of back stairs at the back of my home (while Herman sat nearby overseeing the job) some friends from the city three hundred miles away drove up and stopped. We talked for a while outside and then I invited them inside for a cool drink. When they were ready to leave, we said our "take it easies" and they got into their car to leave while I went back to work on the stairs. I was engrossed in the project when about an hour later their car pulled back up in my driveway. My friend's wife got out of the car, opened the back door and reached in and removed Herman from the back window ledge where he was still sound asleep. They had gotten all the way to Keene Valley - a distance of twenty miles, before they noticed Herman lying on the back window ledge. While we were visiting, he had crawled through the open front window and onto the back window ledge and fallen asleep. Had he decided to take his nap on the back floor of the car instead of the window ledge, he might have made it all the way to Broadway.

Herman's prowess as a hunter was comparable to that of other cats but he was strictly a sportsman type hunter, hunting for only the sport and not for food. He lacked the killer instinct and all the game he captured was released to be enjoyed again at a later date. Perhaps this might have been due to the fact that none of the squirrels or chipmunks smelled or tasted like Tender Vittles. A number of times I saw Herman carrying chipmunks or squirrels by the neck like a cat carries its kittens. He would play with them until he lost interest in the game and then watch them run off into the woods. I am quite sure a squirrel psychiatrist could have set up a rewarding practice treating all the squirrels that had been subjected to Herman's hunting escapades. I could swear I once saw a squirrel wave at Herman from where he was sitting on a branch of a tree as Herman walked casually beneath. Smokey often accompanied Herman on these hunting excursions out behind the house and I came to believe that some of the older squirrels and chipmunks learned to enjoy the game as much as they did.

If Herman possessed one special attribute, I guess it would have to be his propensity for making friends. I once had a good friend of mine confide in me that Herman couldn't be a cat because he hated cats and liked Herman especially well - therefore by this reasoning, Herman must be a "people" come back in the form of a cat.

Herman went off to Kitty heaven during his fifteenth year. He just went for a walk in the woods behind the house one day and didn't return. A search party in which Smokey participated failed to turn up a trace and I believe Herman just purchased his ticket and boarded a bus for his final destination. I knew he had been feeling poorly and that his steps were not as springy as they once had been.

People often ask about Herman even though he has been gone for five years now. One day if I get a card with a picture of Herman sitting on a large white cloud surrounded by large boxes of Tender Vittles, it would not be any great surprise.

Hermans demise left a void and Smokey exhibited an obvious sense of loss. She searched the woods behind the house often for long periods and I am sure she missed her playing companion more than anyone.

friendship between the two and rarely a day went by that they didn't spend an hour thinking up new games and tricks to play on each other. One of Herman's favorites was to come up behind the couch when the dog was sleeping on the floor in front of the couch. Herman would then leap onto the back of the couch and then jump off landing on the unsuspecting dog. This would be followed by ten or fifteen minutes of frantic play action while they rolled and raced around the living room, often with Herman's head held firmly but gently in Smokey's mouth while the cat held on for dear life with both feet around the dog's neck. They never once hurt each other and it was nearly always Herman who decided the allotted time for playing was up and it was time to get back to the serious business of sleeping or eating.

On those rare occasions that Herman found himself in distress, Smokey was on hand to protect him or to lend a sympathetic ear. When Herman was going through the bad times with the daily baths, Smokey exhibited much concern over Herman's painful distress howls and I am sure that had anyone tried to do Herman harm, Smokey would have taken proper steps to defend him.

Herman once took a trip without ever being aware of it. Once while working on a set of back stairs at the back of my home (while Herman sat nearby overseeing the job) some friends from the city three hundred miles away drove up and stopped. We talked for a while outside and then I invited them inside for a cool drink. When they were ready to leave, we said our "take it easies" and they got into their car to leave while I went back to work on the stairs. I was engrossed in the project when about an hour later their car pulled back up in my driveway. My friend's wife got out of the car, opened the back door and reached in and removed Herman from the back window ledge where he was still sound asleep. They had gotten all the way to Keene Valley - a distance of twenty miles, before they noticed Herman lying on the back window ledge. While we were visiting, he had crawled through the open front window and onto the back window ledge and fallen asleep. Had he decided to take his nap on the back floor of the car instead of the window ledge, he might have made it all the way to Broadway.

    Herman's prowess as a hunter was comparable to that of other cats but he was strictly a sportsman type hunter, hunting for only the sport and not for food. He lacked the killer instinct and all the game he captured was released to be enjoyed again at a later date. Perhaps this might have been due to the fact that none of the squirrels or chipmunks smelled or tasted like Tender Vittles. A number of times I saw Herman carrying chipmunks or squirrels by the neck like a cat carries its kittens. He would play with them until he lost interest in the game and then watch them run off into the pulling the bear down the long trail from the top of the mountain. I was yelling "Mommy, Mommy come see the bear" and my mother came rushing out to see what all the commotion was about.

I don't know why I decided that my old tom cat, who was inside sleeping behind the wood stove, should bee the bear, but while they were talking outside, I entered the house and picked up the sleeping cat - which was nearly as large as I was, and took him outside and sat him on top of the bear. He awoke like someone had just shot him into the air from a cannon and let out an ungodly howl. It was about a hundred yards from the apple tree under which the bear was lying to the edge of the woods, and the tom cat made the trip in a couple of seconds without touching the ground more than three or four times - it seemed. I stood there wide-eyed watching the big cat fly across the meadow, his hair standing straight out on his back. Everyone else had a good laugh but the cat sure didn't think it was very funny.

The cat didn't return to the house for three days. I can still see the reproachful look the cat gave me when it finally walked back into the living room.

THE AGE OLD QUESTION
By Fran Betters

(A philosophical discussion of the world's most important question, by the world's most advanced thinkers - namely fisherman)

A couple of years back, a small group of fisherman, myself included, were discussing philosophy when our elder and most advanced thinker asked the one question that has been asked since the beginning of time. It is asked by small children when they first begin to question life and it is asked all through life by those of all ages right up to the time of their demise from life. The question is "why?".

Now this question has many answers depending on what the question relates to, but in our discussion, we did not deal with specifics but only with the question itself. Now you may ask why we would attempt to discuss such a far reaching and all encompassing question, and the answer of course, is "why not?" (This incidentally, was the second most asked question but we opted to discuss this at another time).

In attempting to answer the question "why?", we must first consider why the question is asked and why it is important to know. There are many who claim to know "why" and often they are given the name "experts" but they often know less about the question than about the answers they give. Why we would even consult them is another dimension of the question that our group can discuss later. Again, you the reader, may wonder why it is so important that we should ask such a question. I could very well answer this but why should I since it is the question "why" that we are concerned with and not the answer.

I must confess that those present at that little gathering were curious to know why our elder and most advanced thinker should ask such a question, but we could only ask "why?" without attempting to answer for that would have meant not playing by the rules.

Ask not why I have written of this important question for I know not why. Why it should be given a full page in this book is another dimension to the question. Come to think about it, why the hell did you read this anyway?

THE MINNOW THIEF
By Fran Betters

A few years back, in the early stages of operating a Sport shop along the banks of the AuSable river, I decided it would be a good idea to add Minnows (small bait fish) to my store of tackle available to fisherman. Even though I specialize in fly fishing equipment, the few extra dollars the minnows would bring would be helpful in paying the bills.

Since there was a small spring freshet that ran through the little gully beside my shop, it would be no problem building a wooden cage in the center of the little spring hole that would provide running clean water for the minnow's sustenance. It only took a few hour's labor to build the cage with screen windows allowing water to filter through, and a wooden cover that sat securely over the top. A few minnow traps set in the river to capture the minnows and transport them to my cage and I was in business.

All went well for the first couple of weeks until one morning I was out to check my supply of minnows. As I approached the cage, I noticed that the cover had been lifted off - and further checking revealed that most of my minnows had been stolen. At first, I thought that some of my friends had just borrowed some of my minnows and wondered why they hadn't replaced the cover. I replenished my supply of minnows from the river and all was well until a few days later, the same thing occurred. This time, I was a little annoyed since setting traps and attending them is both time consuming and work. Right after replenishing he minnows again, I decided I would keep and eye on the cage and try to catch the culprit and give them a piece of my mind. I reasoned that whoever was taking the minnow must be taking them early in the morning so before I opened my shop the next morning I awoke at the crack of dawn and went down to the little brook to check. The cage cover was in position and as I turned to go back to my shop, I heard a rustle in the brush alongside the little stream. Stopping in my tracks, I peered intently towards the leaves and then took a couple steps forwards in an attempt to see who was hiding in the bushes. As I got closer, I saw a face peering out at me through the parted leaves. It was a large mother Raccoon and she was waiting patiently for me to leave so she could go fishing for minnows. Watching her, I went back to the cage and removed the cover and taking the minnow scoop, dipped out about a dozen minnows and went over and dumped them on the ground in front of Mother Coon. For a minute she stood her ground and then cautiously took a few steps forward and still looking at me, picked up one of the minnows. Admonishing Mrs. Raccoon to stay away from the cage, I then went back to my shop and found a latch and hook which I proceeded to secure the cover of the cage to prevent further pilferage.

Thereafter, whenever I went down to the cage, or replenished the supply of minnows, I would dip out about a dozen and leave them at the side of the stream where Mother Coon would often be waiting, probably trying to figure out how to unlatch that cage.

OLD BROWNIE AND DAD
By Fran Betters

From my childhood days until just past thirty, I can recall the many times I've seen my father return from the stream with huge fish, but the one grand daddy of them all was the one he caught just before he passed away in 1964. It was an exceptionally large brown trout which both my father and I gave the name "Old Brownie". Old Brownie held the Houdini award for his ability to escape and for a period of four years, my father and I lost that fish a good half dozen times. Brownie lived in the large pool just across the street and down over the bank from our house in what my father called the step rock pool. Alongside the large pool was a large boulder where one could sit with feet resting on a lower level comfortably like sitting in a chair. After many a morning's fishing, my father and I would sit on this boulder and reflect for awhile on the morning's fishing; or sit in the evening and watch the mayflies hatching out on the river and watch them mate in the air and then lay their eggs on the water, and then watch the trout in the pool begin to feed on the insects. From this pool we had taken many nice trout, some as large as four pounds but it was after one particularly heavy rain, when the river was rising, that my father first hooked Old Brownie. Dad was fishing a large Royal Wulff dry fly about nine o'clock on a saturday morning and I was fishing across from him slightly downstream on the opposite side of the river.

He shouted to me that he was onto a big fish and I stopped fishing to watch the battle. It was like he was hooked onto a large log as the fish started downstream with my father in close pursuit putting as much pressure on the slender shaft of the fly rod as he dared. I will never forget the sight of that fish as it swam past me and into the fast surging currents of the quickly rising stream. It's tail was partly out of the water and the spots on it's side were as big as silver dollars. Both my father and I had caught trout weighing up to six pounds before but this fish was larger than anything we had caught on a fly rod. The fish began to put distance between itself and my father, and when it got into the heavy currents, there was no holding it. My father was seventy then and had emphysema. Even his experience in handling large fish with a fly rod was no match, and he was unable to keep up with the fish in the heavy currents. The fish broke off about a hundred feet farther downstream. This was in early June of that year and it was not until early september that either of us saw Old Brownie again. I was fishing the same pool one evening just before dark and hooked a small trout about eight inches long. Since daylight was quickly fading and some good trout were rising, I was anxious to get the small trout in and release it so I could resume casting to the larger fish. I was bringing the fish quickly towards me when I saw this large tail and swirl behind the small trout. Before I could react, Old Brownie grabbed the small fish in his mouth and headed out into the heavier currents. I fought him for a good five minutes with just him holding onto the small fish with its teeth. Whether he couldn't let go or wouldn't, I don't know, but finally the small fish came out of Old Brownie's mouth and I brought it the rest of the way in. Old Brownie's teeth had ripped most of the skin from just behind the head back to it's head. I was still shaking from the excitement when I put the small fish in my creel, went up the bank and walked across the street to my home. I showed the smaller trout to my father explaining what had happened and he told me that he had the same thing happen a couple of times with larger fish taking a trout he had hooked.

The next season both my father and I hooked Old Brownie but he always managed to do just the right thing to escape. The following year, I again had a brief encounter with Brownie but he quickly put a large boulder between us as he headed downstream and broke off. Neither of us saw him again that year.

It was not until the next year in June that Old Brownie and Dad had staged their final engagement. My father's emphysema had gotten worse but he decided to venture down over the bank to fish the step pool. That particular morning I had something to do elsewhere and did not accompany my father to the river when he left the house about seven in the morning. I arrived back about ten and my mother expressed her concern that Dad wasn't back yet and I started down to the river to check on him. Half way down the steep path that led to the river, I met my Dad coming up. He was tired and his breathing was difficult but what he was partly carrying and partly dragging added a gleam to his eyes and when he lifted Old Brownie with the large Royal Wulff still embedded in his jaw, It was anticlimactic of all fishing years behind my father. It was one of the happiest moments of my life as I secretly hoped that my father could catch Old Brownie before his fishing days came to an end. We took pictures of Old Brownie, weighed and measured him. Old Brownie was twenty seven and a half inches long and weighed seven pounds eleven ounces. It was the largest brown trout my father had ever taken on the AuSable river, either on fly or bait and I have never taken a trout of that size since that time, nor have I seen one taken. It was a fitting tribute to my father's skill as a fly fisherman, and the stream he loved so well had given him its final farewell gift to take with him on his journey to another river. He passed away a few months later and I am sure that at least once in those final days, he must have relived that final encounter with Old Brownie.